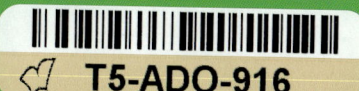

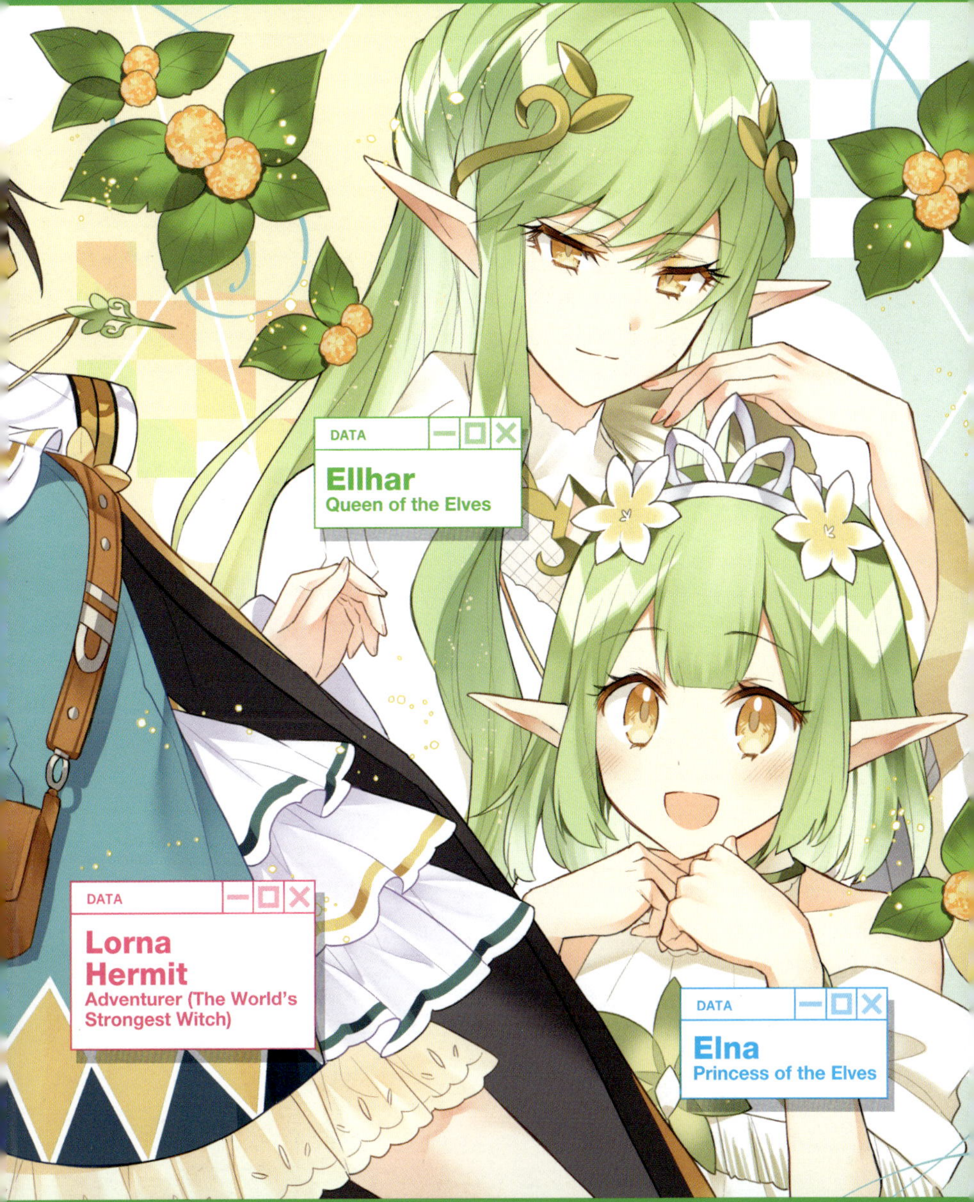
DATA
Ellhar
Queen of the Elves
DATA
Lorna Hermit
Adventurer (The World's Strongest Witch)
DATA
Elna
Princess of the Elves

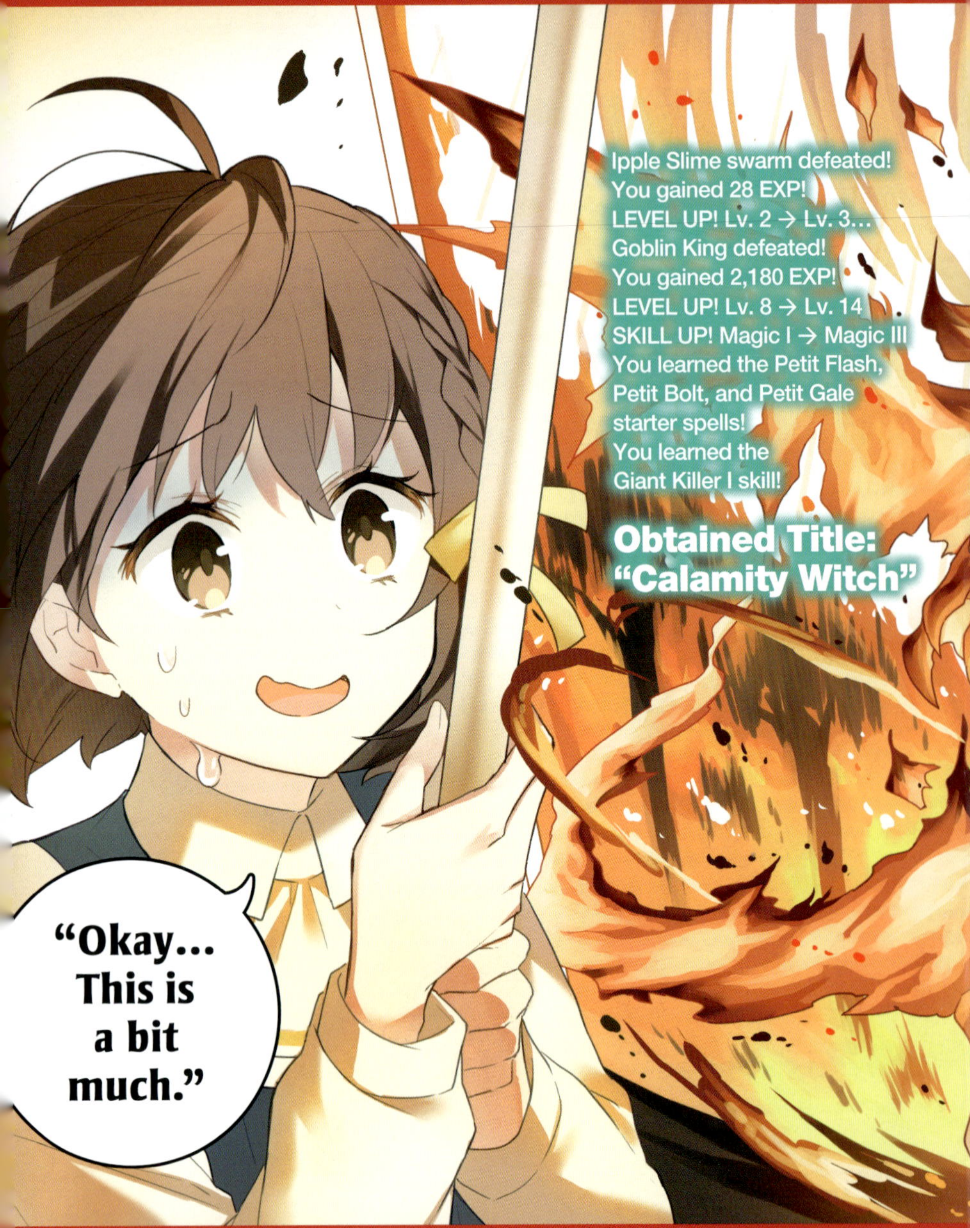
Ipple Slime swarm defeated!
You gained 28 EXP!
LEVEL UP! Lv. 2 → Lv. 3…
Goblin King defeated!
You gained 2,180 EXP!
LEVEL UP! Lv. 8 → Lv. 14
SKILL UP! Magic I → Magic III
You learned the Petit Flash, Petit Bolt, and Petit Gale starter spells!
You learned the Giant Killer I skill!
Obtained Title: "Calamity Witch"
"Okay… This is a bit much."

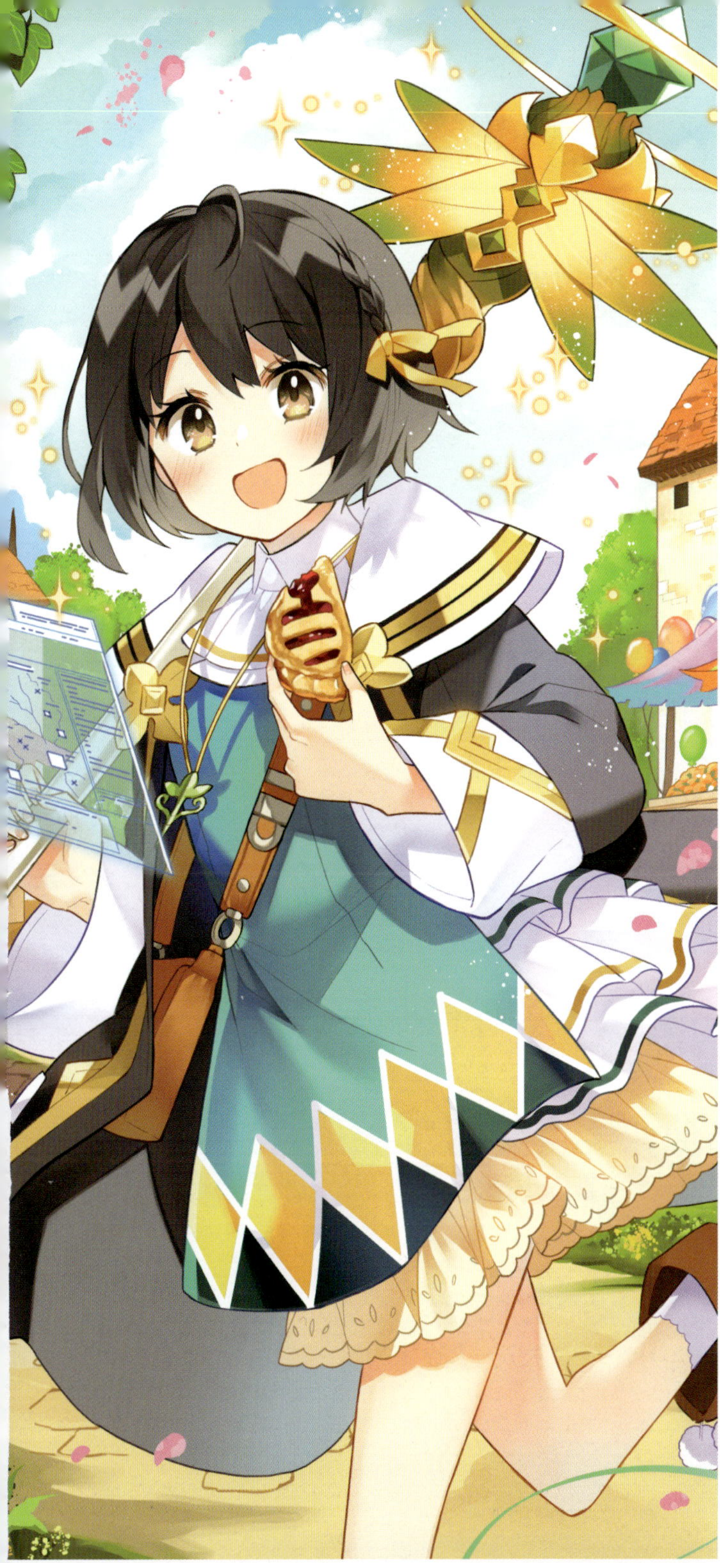

The World's Strongest Witch

I'm Starting My Free Life in a World Where Only I Can See the Online Strategy Guide

1

Mochimaru Sakaki

Illustration by
riritto

YEN ON
NEW YORK

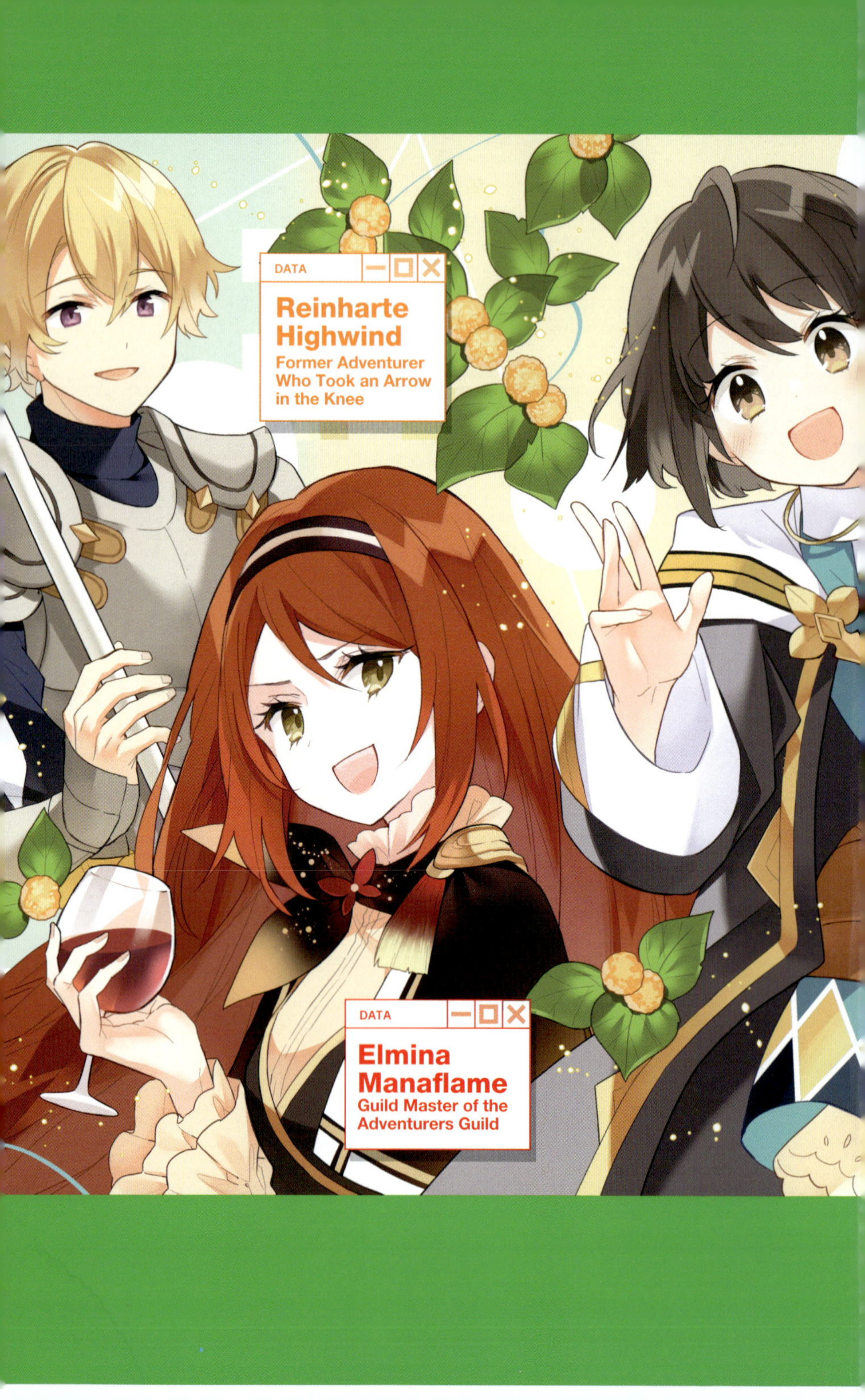
DATA
Reinharte Highwind
Former Adventurer Who Took an Arrow in the Knee
DATA
Elmina Manaflame
Guild Master of the Adventurers Guild

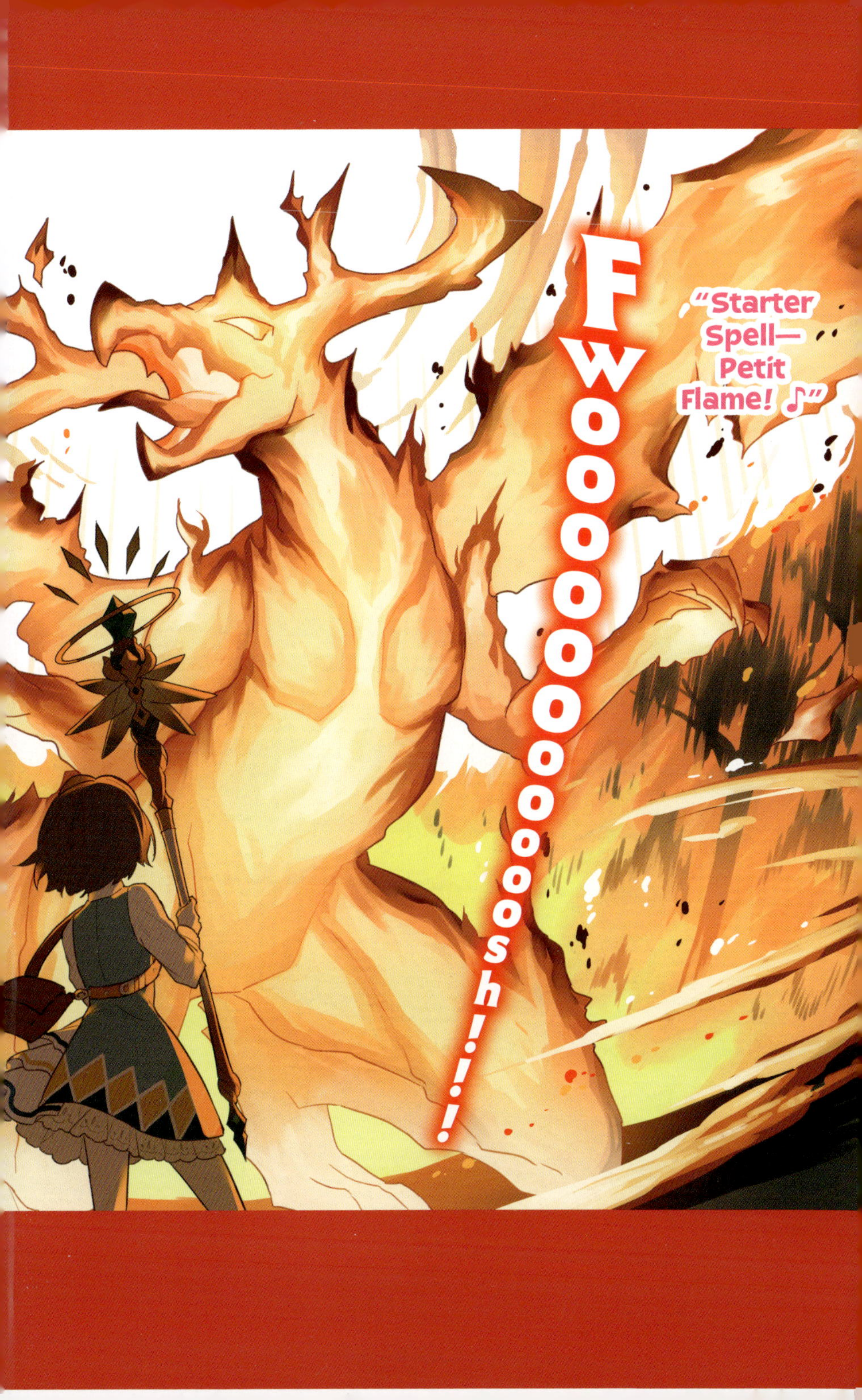
"Starter Spell—Petit Flame! ♪"
Fwooooooooooooosh!!!!

Obtained Title: "Calamity Witch"!

The World's Strongest Witch:
I'm Starting My Free Life in a World Where Only
I Can See the Online Strategy Guide

Contents	Event Guide	Maps
Enemy List	Item List	

Chapter 1	I Tried Using the Internet!	001
Chapter 2	I Tried Getting My Hands on a Legendary Staff!	013
Chapter 3	I Tried Taking on the Lord of the Woods!	031
Chapter 4	I Tried Healing a Person in Distress!	045
Chapter 5	I Tried Taking the Adventurers Exam!	057
Chapter 6	I Tried Exploring a Dungeon!	075
Chapter 7	I Tried Fighting the Dungeon Boss!	083
Chapter 8	I Became an Adventurer!	107
Chapter 9	I Gathered an Infinite Number of Herbs!	115
Chapter 10	I Went to the Elven Village!	127
Chapter 11	I Tried Making Elven Nostrum!	139
Chapter 12	I Put an End to the Bad Guy's Ambitions!	149
Chapter 13	I Became the Savior of the World!	159
Chapter 14	I Brought Back Souvenirs!	171
Chapter 15	I Left on a Journey!	183
Chapter 16	Epilogue	195
Side Story	Registering to Be an Adventurer	207
Afterword		213

DATA — VOLUME 1

THE WORLD'S STRONGEST WITCH
I'm Starting My Free Life in a World Where Only I Can See the Online Strategy Guide

Mochimaru Sakaki

Cover art by riritto   **Translation by** Phil Charbonneau

This book is a work of fiction. Names, characters, places, and incidents are the product of the author's imagination or are used fictitiously. Any resemblance to actual events, locales, or persons, living or dead, is coincidental.

SEKAI SAIKYO NO MAJO, HAJIMEMASHITA ~WATASHI DAKE "KORYAKU-SITE" WO MIRERU SEKAI DE JIYU NI IKIMASU~ vol. 1
©2022 Mochimaru Sakaki, riritto/SQUARE ENIX CO., LTD.
First published in Japan in 2022 by SQUARE ENIX CO., LTD. English translation rights arranged with SQUARE ENIX CO., LTD. and Yen Press, LLC through Tuttle-Mori Agency, Inc.

English translation © 2025 by Yen Press, LLC

Yen Press, LLC supports the right to free expression and the value of copyright. The purpose of copyright is to encourage writers and artists to produce the creative works that enrich our culture.

The scanning, uploading, and distribution of this book without permission is a theft of the author's intellectual property. If you would like permission to use material from the book (other than for review purposes), please contact the publisher. Thank you for your support of the author's rights.

Yen On
150 West 30th Street, 6th Floor
New York, NY 10001

Visit us at yenpress.com ★ facebook.com/yenpress ★ twitter.com/yenpress
yenpress.tumblr.com ★ instagram.com/yenpress

First Yen On Edition: August 2025
Edited by Yen On Editorial: Emma McClain
Designed by Yen Press Design: Madelaine Norman

Yen On is an imprint of Yen Press, LLC.
The Yen On name and logo are trademarks of Yen Press, LLC.

The publisher is not responsible for websites (or their content)
that are not owned by the publisher.

Library of Congress Cataloging-in-Publication Data is available.

ISBNs: 979-8-8554-1435-6 (paperback)
979-8-8554-1436-3 (ebook)

1 3 5 7 9 10 8 6 4 2

LSC-C

Printed in the United States of America

THE WORLD'S STRONGEST WITCH

I'm Starting My Free Life in a World Where Only I Can See the Online Strategy Guide

Mochimaru Sakaki

Illustration by
riritto

Chapter 1　I Tried Using the Internet!

"I can't believe I've been kicked out with nothing more than the clothes on my back…"

To get right to the point: Lorna Hermit was standing alone in the middle of a forest. She had no weapons. No armor. No money. It was not a good state of affairs to find oneself in. Especially not in a monster-infested forest.

What had happened was simple: Lorna's family had left her to die.

"What is the meaning of this, Lorna?!"

"You've manifested an incredibly weak skill of the lowest possible rank! How could you bring shame to your family like this?!"

"Your brothers all have B-Rank or higher skills. Why can't you be more like them?"

Her mind was filled with memories of the skill appraisal ceremony from the day before. She recalled the insults hurled at her by her family, the jeers of the other attendees…

Lorna had been born into the illustrious House of Guugelheit, a line of warriors. Her father was a margrave.

And yet she had manifested an SSS-Rank skill. Not only was it ranked S—a letter far lower than what was often thought to be the lowest letter possible, G—it had three of them! That clearly meant it was even worse! This was an unpardonable sin for a member of the Guugelheit family.

The people of this world were judged according to the rank of their skills, and that rank was said to correspond directly to how much they were favored by the gods.

"Get out of here! You are hereby banished from our family! You are not to use our family name ever again!"

So it was for that reason Lorna was thrown into the woods like a common criminal.

"I can't believe I'm going to die all alone out here..."

Lorna assumed the only reason they hadn't killed her on the spot was to avoid getting their hands dirty and sullying the lineage with a criminal record.

Yes, her situation was dire, but Lorna was grateful to have made it out alive at least.

She sighed as she opened her status screen.

■ **Lorna Hermit, Lv. 1**
HP: 10/10
MP: 12/12
ATK: 3
DEF: 4 (+5)
M-ATK: 9
MIND: 9
SPD: 4 (+2)
LUCK: 8

◆ **Equipment**
Weapon: None

Chapter 1: I Tried Using the Internet!

> Armor: Cloth Dress (G)
> Armor: Leather Shoes (G)
>
> ◆ Skills
> Internet (SSS)
> Magic I (G)
>
> ◆ Titles
> The Abandoned One

Lorna Hermit, Level 1...

At some point, her family name had been changed to her mother's maiden name: Hermit.

The fact that she had been cast out of the Guugelheit family was really starting to hit home. Worse, she was only at Level 1 and had no useful equipment or skills. At this rate, she could forget about ever leaving the woods; she would probably get murdered by the first weak monster she ran into.

"If only I could figure out what this 'Internet' skill does..."

Not that she had much faith in an SSS-Rank skill—the weakest of the weak.

"Well, first things first...I have to try to get to the nearest town alive."

Just as Lorna steeled her resolve and began to cautiously make her way through the forest...

Boi-oing!

...a small shadow descended on her from the trees above.

"Wh-what the—?! Wait...It's just a slime."

It had scared her half to death. She figured it had jumped down from the tree in an attempt to land on her face and suffocate her. She'd heard that the Ipple Slimes in the Ipple Woods hunted that way.

"Well, as long as it's just a slime, I'm sure even I can handle it... right?"

Lorna had been studying and practicing magic her whole life. And while it might have been only a G-Rank skill, she had learned Magic I, which allowed her to use beginner spells. And so...

"Starter Spell—Petit Ice!" she timidly incanted.

A magic circle formed in front of her palms. Tiny shards of ice emerged from the circle and gingerly collided with the Slime.

"No effect?!"

The slime was entirely unfazed by her attack. It jiggled as it continued to charge toward her.

"Th-this thing's strong!"

It wasn't, of course. Lorna was just weak. At Level 1 and without so much as a staff, defeating the slime with spells was going to be a tall order.

"...Looks like I've got no choice. I'm going to have to use it."

Lorna made up her mind. She thrust out her palms in front of her and cried out.

"I summon you—INTERNET!"

This was the name of the SSS-Rank skill she had manifested only one day prior. The time had finally come to activate it.

Particles of light gathered in front of Lorna's palms until they formed a translucent board. And then...

"Goooo, Internet!" she called out.

She pointed at the slime and directed her Internet skill to attack it. But nothing happened.

"……"

A moment of uncomfortable silence passed. The internet merely floated, unresponsive, glowing with a white ambient light.

Lorna awkwardly cleared her throat. Then, after regaining her composure—

"INTERNET KICK!!!"

—she booted the slime into the air.

The creature, which had likely been distracted by the glow of the internet, was unable to avoid the attack. It smacked into a nearby tree with a splat and died.

The slime vanished in a puff of smoke, leaving behind a small gem—crystallized mana.

Defeated Ipple Slime! You gained 4 EXP!
LEVEL UP! Lv. 1 ➔ Lv. 2

Lorna stared at the text that had appeared before her eyes.

"Hah! Ah-ha-ha…! So this is the power of Internet!"

But as soon as the words had left her mouth, she felt hollow inside.

"Whyyy…? Why did I have to manifest such a weird, pointless skill?"

Not that any of this came as a surprise. What could she expect from a skill even weaker than G-Rank? Lorna had hoped that if she summoned it in front of a monster, *something* would happen. But it seemed she'd been wrong.

"It's definitely not a combat skill…"

Lorna wasn't particularly hungry for the thrill of battle. But it would have been nice to have some kind of skill to use for self-protection.

Then again, a combat skill with a rank as low as SSS probably wouldn't do much to prevent her grisly demise in these woods.

"An Ipple Slime gem… I think one of these is worth ten shil, right?"

She proceeded to claim her spoils, though the most ten shil would get her was a helping of bread crusts. Even the cheapest of accommodations cost one thousand shil. At this rate, it looked like she would be sleeping outside.

"Urgh… What a cruel world."

Tears welled up in Lorna's eyes as she put the monster's gem in her bag.

"I wish I could at least figure out how to use this internet thing," she said, poking at the glowing screen.

"…?!"

Suddenly—*click*—something on the screen changed.

When her finger touched the long, thin rectangle in the middle of the screen, a panel with letters appeared. It almost looked like a puzzle.

She had never seen any of the letters before. But somehow, she understood them.

"So…does it want me to use these letters to make words? Let's see… Maybe I need to put in a password or something."

Unfortunately, nothing came to mind.

"Well, I won't get anywhere without trying."

She decided to begin by typing the word *internet*.

"I…N…T…E… Uh… I wonder which one of these is supposed to be the R? Oh, here it— Whoops! I didn't mean to hit that one! How am I supposed to erase letters on this thing…? I guess I'm going to have to erase it all and start over… Hold on. I can't remember what I did to bring up the panel with all those letters anymore. What was it again?"

This continued for about ten minutes, until finally…

"Phew, there we go!"

The letters she had typed floated proudly in the middle of the screen.

internet

Satisfied, she tapped the ENTER button.

"Whoa, the screen changed! Looks like I guessed right!"

On her very first try. Impressive.

Boy, I'm doing great today!
She could feel the excitement well up inside her.

"But…now a whole bunch of *other* letters have shown up. It looks like a list of book titles or something… Th-there are so many!"

All the titles seemed to have something to do with the internet. Lorna guessed that it was showing her a list of books related to the word she had just entered.

"Hmm, let's see… What about this one? Uh… Wiki…pedi…a? It says 'The internet is a system of com…put…ers that uses the internet…proto-call sweet? …to communicate between networks and something, something…' Okay, I have no idea what any of this means, but I can see the word *encyclopedia* here… So I guess Internet is like a library skill."

It was a tool for gathering information. Suddenly, it made sense why nothing had happened when Lorna activated it.

I was really hoping for a combat skill I could use to protect myself, but…I guess if I'm going on an adventure, I'll need as much info as I can get.

Thinking it over, this skill of hers didn't seem so bad after all.

"All right! The first thing I want is…a map of the Ipple Woods."

If she couldn't find her way out of the woods, Lorna was practically guaranteed to meet a gruesome end. But maps were valuable items. She didn't expect it would be so easy to look one up.

"Oh well. No harm in trying, I guess. I… P… P… L… E… Wait, how do I put a space between the words…? Oh, it must be this bar down here. W… O… O… D… S. There!"

She entered the letters into the internet just as she had a moment ago. Once again, a list of titles appeared on the screen.

The one at the very top of the list caught her eye.

Ipple Woods Map—Etalia Wiki Guides

"…Wiki Guide? What's that?"

She wasn't sure what the words meant, but perhaps she would find a simple map of the area. She touched the title and—*click*—the screen changed.

"...I-it worked! It's a map!"

There was no doubt about it—the page before her showed a map of the Ipple Woods. It was so intricate that she could hardly believe it was a map of a forest.

"Th-there's no way! What in the world...? I've never seen a map with so much detail before!"

It showed areas of the forest without paths and even came with illustrations so elaborate they looked like pictures of the real thing. It was way more detailed than the map of the domain she'd seen back in her childhood home.

Hold on… Something like this could be really bad news…

The Guugelheit domain was on the border of a neighboring country. A map this detailed was equivalent to a state secret. A regular person like Lorna probably wasn't even supposed to see it.

But this is a matter of life and death, so… Okay! I'm doing it! I'm gonna look!

Lorna peeked at the map while cautiously keeping an eye on her surroundings.

"I should be right around here, but… Wha—? What's this marker?"

She noticed some words written at the bottom of the map.

■ **Map: Ipple Woods**
Item #4: 500 shil

They seemed to indicate that there were five hundred shil nearby.

Wh-what? Whoa, whoa, whoa… Come on. There's no way the map knows something like that, right?

But suspicions aside, Lorna had zero shil to her name. If there was money to be had, she wanted it.

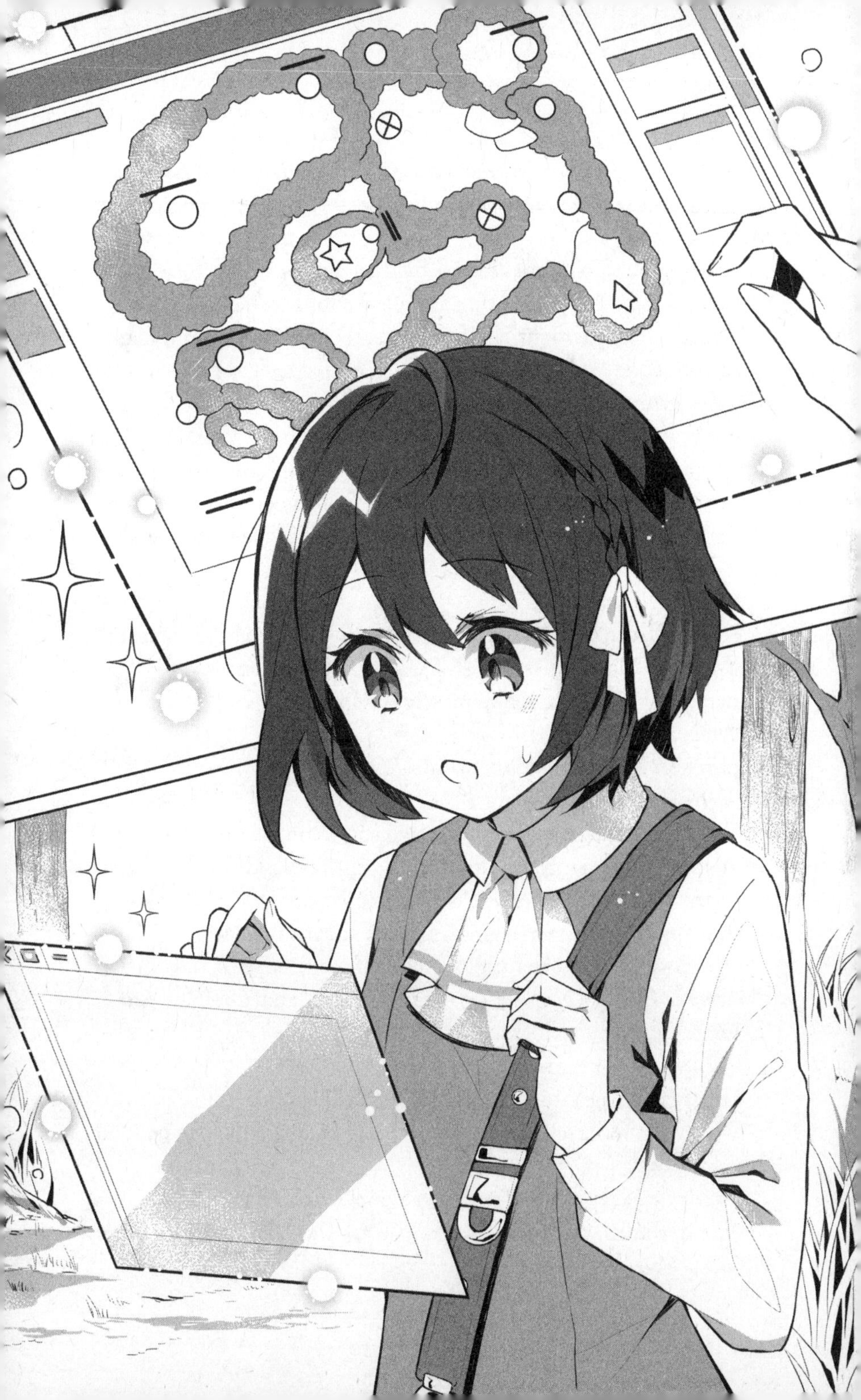

W-well, I guess it might be worth checking out. Besides, I need to find out how accurate the map is, Lorna thought, trying to justify her actions.

She wandered to some nearby bushes, and pushing them aside, she found something glittering among the foliage—a small coin.

"Th-the map was right…! There's exactly five hundred shil here!"

For someone as dead broke as Lorna, even a measly five hundred shil was cause for celebration. And yet…

"How did it know something like that? What the heck *is* this internet thing…?"

The internet seemed to know not only that someone had dropped money in the middle of the woods, but also the exact amount they had dropped. Was that even possible?

…This is seriously creepy.

Perhaps Lorna had underestimated the power of the internet's knowledge. More terrifying still was that the information it contained didn't seem limited to merely the Ipple Woods.

"Map…List…?"

Lorna timidly touched the words.

"Wh-what is—?"

The screen shifted to display a page containing what appeared to be maps of every single location in the entire world. This included even the deepest parts of as-yet-unexplored dungeons. There were even maps of hidden passageways inside the royal palace.

That was when Lorna noticed the following page titles: *List of Important People*, *Complete List of Equipment*, and *Complete List of Skills*.

Her own skill began to terrify her.

"Th-this internet thing is…unbelievable."

That was underselling it. Something had finally dawned on Lorna.

There's…no way this skill could be worse than a G-Rank skill.

The B-Rank skills like Magic Sword that her brothers were

always boasting about, and even the A-Rank skills she had heard about in rumors—all paled in comparison to Internet.

"This skill... It must allow me to tap into the wisdom of the gods."

What was written on this screen was the very truth of the world. It was like a divine bookcase that contained all knowledge.

"That's what this is... That's the power of the internet."

Lorna swallowed the lump in her throat.

If I can learn to use my Internet skill fully, then...

There was no telling how much knowledge and power she could access. Just thinking about it made her tremble. But then...

"Lorna... You should live your life freely. The way you want to."

...her mother's dying words suddenly came back to her.

When Lorna was a child, her mother would often regale her with tales of the outside world. She loved her mother's stories and always wished that one day, she, too, would be able to see the world for herself.

But she was the daughter of a noble, and she had obligations. She would never be allowed to venture out on her own. Her father had forbidden her from ever leaving their estate, and she had grown up believing that, just as her mother before her, she would spend her entire life within the confines of the family home.

But now, with the power of the internet at her disposal, maybe, just maybe, she could live a life like the heroes in her beloved stories—a life of freedom. A life where she could travel to all sorts of places, eat all sorts of yummy foods, meet all sorts of interesting people...

As these visions of her new life grew grander and grander still, Lorna's heart began to pound in her chest.

"I think that, maybe...it's for the best that I was kicked out before I learned about the power of the internet."

If Lorna had understood the limitless powers at her disposal before being cast out, the Guugelheit family would surely have locked her away and used her as a tool.

In the worst-case scenario, everyone in the world might have come after her for her power. She could have been kidnapped or assassinated... It could have caused wars!

This skill of hers was simply *that* amazing.

"W-well anyway...I should look up more stuff...more and more and more!"

Knowledge was power. There was still so much she needed to know.

Brimming with energy and impatience, Lorna touched the screen once again, and...

"Uh. What's this weird thing that just popped up? An...ad? What's an ad? O-oh geez. How do I go back to the last page...? Uh, let me see. Maybe I have to tap this X? Ugh, come on! Why is the X so small?! I just... Wh-wha—?! W-w-wait...!"

For some reason, the so-called ads began to multiply and multiply until...

"...N-no! No, no, no...!"

Lorna stood in complete shock.

Something new was written on the screen, right in front of her face.

[!] CRITICAL SYSTEM FAILURE [!]
Warning: Tap the UPDATE button below to install the latest repair software. Your files will be deleted in 230 seconds.

"Th-the internet... It's broken?!"

Chapter 2 I Tried Getting My Hands on a Legendary Staff!

"Pheeew. Looks like internet's fixed now."

Some time had passed since the internet broke down.

Lorna wasn't sure why, but turning the screen off and then on again seemed to fix whatever the problem was. Once again, she was able to use the internet without any issues.

"I can't believe how easy it is to break the internet... I should be careful when using it."

Lorna sighed in relief and began carefully tapping the screen once more.

After getting it back up and running, she'd experimented a bit and grown a little more accustomed to how it worked.

She now knew how to open multiple "windows" and turn on "incognito mode" so that no one else could see what she was doing.

"Let's see... According to the internet, there should be a fork in the road... There it is!" Lorna called out as the split in the path came into view.

It was exactly as the internet had foretold. She felt reassured.

I knew it. All the information on the internet really is *true!*

Merely calling it information was doing it a disservice. Most of the details the internet revealed to her were on par with state secrets. It was knowledge only the gods themselves could possess.

I still can't believe it knows things like "monster spawn points" and "trap locations."

Its divine knowledge was helping guide her safely through the woods.

What had at first seemed akin to wandering aimlessly through a hellscape full of demons now felt like a leisurely stroll through the park.

But as was human nature, the moment Lorna felt safe, her thoughts turned to other desires.

"Hmm. I wonder if I can find any more loose change on the ground around here. Five hundred shil isn't going to be enough for an inn, so... Huh?"

As she stared at the Ipple Woods map, two words suddenly caught her eye: SECRET PATH. Secret paths—the kinds one found in dungeons—often led to untold treasure that had been hidden away from the world.

"Maybe if I go all the way down this secret path...I'll find a *bunch* of loose change!"

Trying her best to contain her excitement, Lorna studied the route on the map. And there, at its end...

■ **Map: Ipple Woods**
◇ **Secret Clearing**
Item: Staff of World Tree (SSS)

...was something far more amazing than she had been expecting.

Uh... What? World Tree? So this staff is made from the World Tree or something? Why's something like that just lying around in my neck of the woods?

It was so amazing, in fact, that Lorna was having trouble wrapping her mind around it. And what's more, this staff was *also* SSS-Rank.

H-hold on a minute... There's no way a staff with a crazy name like that is worse than a G-Rank staff. SSS-Rank must be at least one rank above A…right?

And if there was something Lorna didn't know, what better time to search the internet?

She perused the Wiki Guide for a bit and quickly found her answer.

■ Terminology: Ranks
G➔F➔E➔D➔C➔B➔A➔S➔SS➔SSS

The power of equipment and skills is determined by their rank, in the above order.

Incidentally, equipment and skills of Rank S and higher were added during later updates and, as a result, are only found as rewards for higher difficulty content.

When starting the game, A-Rank skills are the highest possible rank attainable through the skill gacha.

"So it was three ranks higher than A this whole time…?"

Who could have imagined?

More importantly, why does S come after A? And why is the next rank after that SS? It's so confusing for no reason. Why not just make it AAA? Or use stars or something?

Lorna wondered what the system's designer must have been thinking. In fact, the resulting confusion had made her father believe she'd brought shame on her family and was the whole reason she'd been chased out of her home. She was a victim of this overcomplicated nonsense!

"Oh well. Anyway… I should check out this secret path."

Everything she had seen on the map so far had turned out to be true, so it seemed practically guaranteed that it was correct about what awaited her at the end of the secret path. And that meant, as impossible as it was to believe, a staff of the highest rank was here, in these woods.

B-but...if it's written on the internet then it must *be true, right?*

The words on the internet were from the gods themselves. There was no way any of it could possibly be a lie.

So Lorna swallowed hard and headed toward the secret path mentioned on the map.

"Uh, let's see... Secret path. It should be here, but..."

The map said the entrance to the path was somewhere around the roots of a giant tree.

Lorna approached the tree and ran her hand along it. When she did, her surroundings warped like ripples on the surface of water.

"Whoa!"

In the blink of an eye, the massive tree disappeared. In its place, a tunnel of greenery appeared. This *had* to be the secret path mentioned on the map.

"I-it's really here... I can't believe the internet knew about this, too!"

She had repeated the same phrase dozens of times already, but she couldn't help it.

"U-um, pardon me. I'm coming in!" she called, stepping into the hidden path with some trepidation.

She nervously walked through the tunnel. And on the other side...

"What...is this place?"

...she found a small forest clearing.

Flowers were blooming here and there. Butterflies fluttered about. A small sapling stood soaking up the sunrays. That was about it. But the spot did have a sacred feeling. Every time Lorna took a breath, it felt like something was sucking the impurities out of her body.

"Hmm, so where exactly is this staff supposed to be...?"

Unlike the loose change she'd found earlier, no spot in particular jumped out at her. She took a look at the internet again and realized she'd missed a section that detailed how to obtain the staff.

■ **Weapon: Staff of World Tree**
◇ **Defeat the guardian found at the Astral Observatory of the Twelve Stars and complete the Star Map Disc to obtain the key words** *Halt, O time. World, be thou beautiful.* **Use the key words in the secret path found in the Ipple Woods to trigger the event and get the staff (no combat encounter).**

"...Huh."
One thing was clear: Lorna had no idea what any of that meant.
"Basically...I just have to say these words, right?"
There was no harm in trying.

"Halt, O time. World, be thou beautiful."

Lorna spoke the words somewhat half-heartedly. But the change that followed was sudden and dramatic.
"Whoa!"
Fwooosh!
A blinding light flooded the forest clearing.
The light slowly began to gather in front of Lorna until it formed the shape of a woman. She almost looked like a spirit out of a fairy tale. In fact, that's *exactly* what she looked like. She had hair like a verdant summer breeze and was wrapped in a white robe wreathed with flowers. Her whole body was so pale it was translucent. Her countenance gave off a sense of divine majesty.
"It is a pleasure to meet you, O child of man. I am the spirit of the World Tree. You may call me Yggdrasil. You have done well in overcoming the Trial of the Twelve Stars."

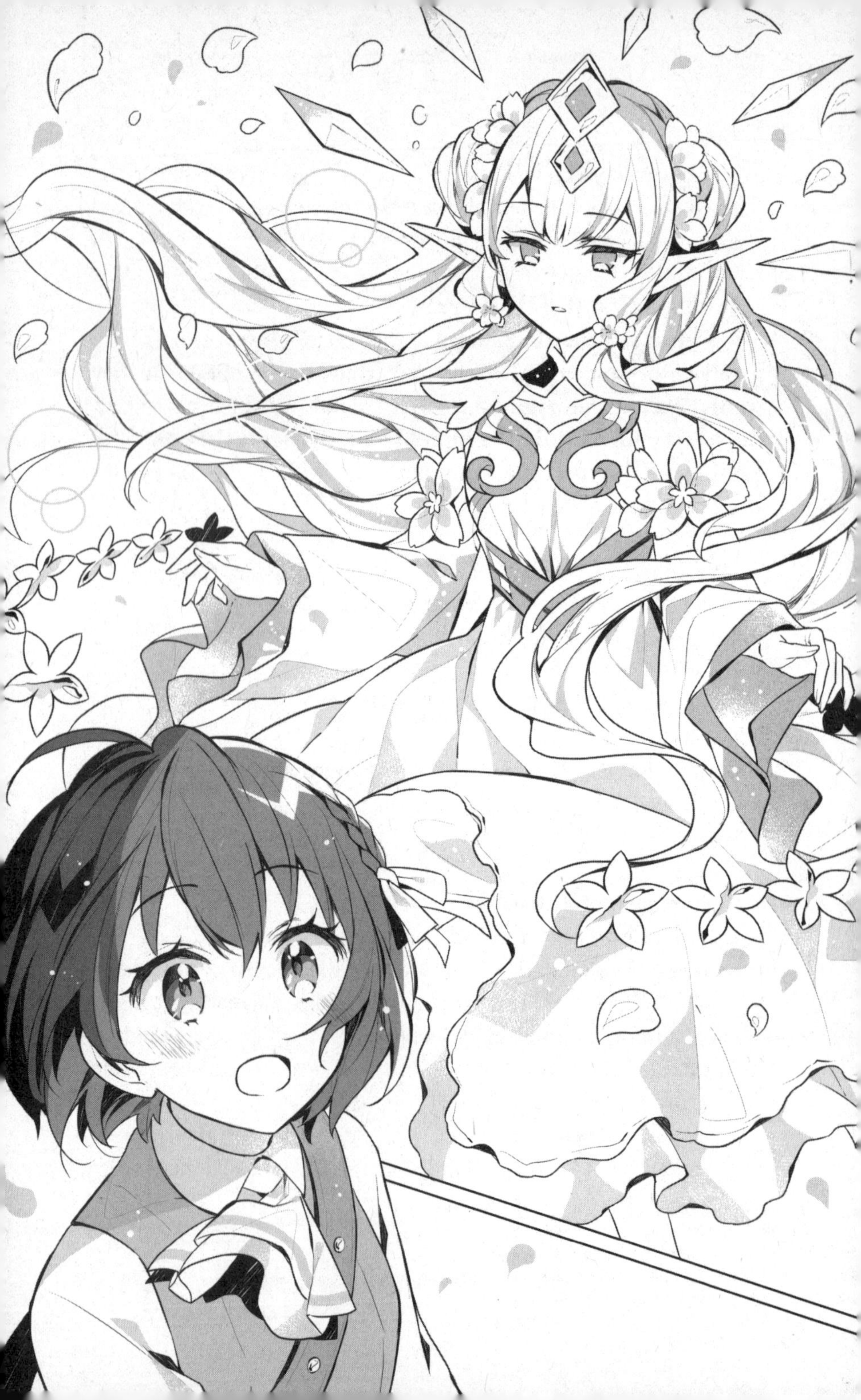

Chapter 2: I Tried Getting My Hands on a Legendary Staff!

* * *

The spirit spoke with a gentle tone. Lorna had never heard a voice so beautiful. It was as clear as spring water.

But something more pressing was taking up Lorna's attention.

...Trial? What trial?

Lorna didn't remember completing any "trial."

Oh dear... I think I might have skipped over a few things.

Lorna began to sweat nervously.

"U-um, well... I, uh..."

"There is no need for you to explain. Only those pure of heart who have overcome the trial can speak the hallowed words."

Oh. Oh no... She is way, way off about me.

Lorna tried to think of a way to explain. But before she could, the woman spoke again.

"You must have had many adventures on your journey to this hallowed place."

Actually, my adventure only started about an hour ago...

"You must have met many people along the way and experienced many a bittersweet parting."

Actually, you're the first person I've met so far...

"It is for these reasons that I am confident I can entrust this child to you."

The moment the woman stopped speaking, the saplings in front of Lorna rustled and formed into the shape of a single staff. Its tip was adorned with an emerald-green gem. One glance was enough to tell that this thing was incredibly powerful.

"This staff—along with this world—I entrust it to you."

"Th-the whole world?!"

Without thinking, Lorna reached up and grabbed hold of the staff.

The spirit smiled gently. She seemed relieved.

"Ah. Finally... Now I can...return to his side..."

"Huh? Whoa, hold on! Where...?!"

But it was too late for Lorna to stop her. In an instant, the lady spirit turned into particles of light and disappeared.

Suddenly a line of text appeared before her.

Obtained Title: "Yggdrasil's Chosen"

"............................"

With no understanding of what had just happened, Lorna was left standing in the clearing, alone once again. Her hands were still shaking as she grasped the imposing staff.

"Sh-should I maybe...*not* have accepted this, or...?"

She hadn't overcome the trial. She hadn't been on any adventures, met any people, or experienced *any* bittersweet partings. Not to mention, being entrusted with the *world* sounded like way too much responsibility.

"Um... What's the return policy on this thing?"

Her question rang out through the empty clearing. But no response came.

Lorna got on her hands and knees and gracefully bowed her head to the ground.

"I'm sorry, I'm sorry, I'm sooo sorryyy! I thought I could just grab the staff and be on my merry way. I didn't think it would be such a big deal!"

Say the key words out loud, *"Ding, ding, ding, you win the prize! Here's a staff!"* *"Whoo-hoo!"* That's the kind of thing Lorna had expected. But the actual transaction had seemed like a pretty serious affair.

What did she even mean when she said she was "entrusting the world" to me? Am I supposed to do something...? I feel like I've been handed a bomb, and now it's my responsibility to take care of it...

Lorna spent a little more time apologizing to the void, then she sighed and said, "...Oh well," and got back up, resuming her usual happy-go-lucky attitude.

"I got the staff I wanted... And this thing's *definitely* strong. Can't get rid of it now."

Her voice was shaky as she spoke, but she ignored it.

"All right, let's see... I should probably take a look at what this thing can do."

She vaguely recalled that the A-Rank Kingdom Sword had an ATK +500 modifier... So an SSS-Rank staff would probably boost her M-ATK by at least eight hundred.

"Nah, no way... Eight hundred is a bit much. The maximum value for a stat is nine hundred and ninety-nine."

Lorna was skeptical, but she couldn't help feeling excited as she took a look at her stats.

■ **Lorna Hermit, Lv. 2**
HP: 14/14
MP: 99,999/18
ATK: 4 (+360)
DEF: 11 (+5)
M-ATK: 13 (+3,600)
MIND: 13
SPD: 8 (+2)
LUCK: 10

◆ **Equipment**
Weapon: Staff of World Tree (SSS)
Armor: Cloth Dress (G)
Armor: Leather Shoes (G)

◆ **Skills**
Internet (SSS)

> Terra Drain (SSS)
> Magic I (G)
>
> ◆ Titles
> The Abandoned One
> Yggdrasil's Chosen

"......"

Was she seeing that right?

She stood in silence, rubbing her eyes before taking another look at her stats screen.

MP: 99,999/18

Uh... I think the stats screen is broken.

The +3,600 modifier to her M-ATK was equally incomprehensible, of course. Her stats were off the charts to an absurd degree.

"W-well, then. It...looks like the cap for stats wasn't nine hundred ninety-nine after all..."

The hand she was using to hold the staff began to shake uncontrollably.

Even court sorcerers only had around five hundred MP. Sitting at almost one hundred thousand MP, Lorna now had two hundred times that.

None of it made any sense to her. One thing was for sure, though: There was no other human alive with this much MP and M-ATK.

"Does this mean...I've become the strongest in the world?"

The staff she'd collected on a whim turned out to be a hundred times more impressive than she could have ever imagined. It was more like a weapon of mass destruction than a staff. It seemed liable to start a war at any moment.

Chapter 2: I Tried Getting My Hands on a Legendary Staff!

"I-it might be a bit late to be asking this question, but uh…just what the heck is this thing?!"

Lorna realized she hadn't yet looked up any information about the staff. So she opened up the internet and typed in *Staff of World Tree*.

■ **Weapon: Staff of World Tree**
Rank: SSS
Type: Staff
Price: 360,000,000,000 shil
Effect: ATK +360, M-ATK +3,600
MP Stock = 99,999
3x MP Usage, 2x Magic Range & Damage

◇ **Equip Skill: Terra Drain (SSS)**
Effect: Absorbs MP from nearby foes.
Terrain Bonus: 2x Damage in forests and meadows.

◇ **Details:** The in-world lore states, "Elven legend foretells that when calamity befalls the land, a chosen one will take up this staff and become the Savior." But since the staff was added as post-game content in a later update, by the time it can be obtained, the catastrophe has already been averted.

This staff is the most broken weapon available and equipping it with any character trivializes the game's balance. It's the kind of overpowered weapon you might expect to see in a light novel.

"…………Huh."

Lorna closed the internet screen.

"…I'm just going to pretend I didn't see any of that."

She worried she'd fall to pieces if she thought about it too deeply.

Lorna wasn't interested in becoming a savior or the most powerful person in the world. All she wanted was to live a life of freedom.

"A-anyway…the sun's probably going to set soon. I guess I'll just sleep outside today," she said, voicing her thoughts in an attempt to clear her mind.

There was no way she would escape the woods by nightfall. And the clearing she'd found looked like a safe place to spend the night. According to the internet, monsters wouldn't attack her here. So with that in mind, she began preparing to make a fire.

She gathered up kindling and some dried leaves into a little pile. Then she pointed the Staff of World Tree at it.

She had tons of MP, so she didn't need to worry about conserving any of it. It was an all-you-can-magic jamboree as far as Lorna was concerned.

"Starter Spell—Petit Flame! ♪" she shouted cheerfully, hoping to create an ember to get her campfire going.

But the next instant…

Fwoooooooooooooosh!!!

"Fuh…FIRE!!!"

…a massive dragon of flames erupted from Lorna's staff.

Lorna stood in complete shock as an all-consuming inferno swirled before her. The trees, the ground, the monsters—whatever the fire touched was incinerated in an instant and turned to ash. It was as though a massive dragon had devoured everything in the area.

Ipple Slime swarm defeated! You gained 28 EXP!
LEVEL UP! Lv. 2 ➔ Lv. 3
Toxibloom swarm defeated! You gained 148 EXP!
LEVEL UP! Lv. 3 ➔ Lv. 5
Green Goblin swarm defeated! You gained 360 EXP!

LEVEL UP! Lv. 5 ➔ Lv. 8
Goblin King defeated! You gained 2,180 EXP!
LEVEL UP! Lv. 8 ➔ Lv. 14
SKILL UP! Magic I ➔ Magic III
You learned the Petit Flash, Petit Bolt, and Petit Gale starter spells!
You learned the Giant Killer I skill!

Obtained Title: "Calamity Witch"

"............................"

As the blaze settled and the smoke cleared, the only thing left in the clearing was the scorched earth beneath Lorna's feet.

Lorna stood in complete disbelief.

After a few moments had passed, she muttered to herself.

"Okay... That was a bit much."

Massive earthquakes rocked the land that day.

The epicenter of the tremendous quakes was the Guugelheit margravate, which contained the Ipple Woods.

Rowser, one of Margrave Brau Guugelheit's sons, ran to his father's side.

"Father!"

"What is it? What's all the commotion?" Brau furrowed his brow in irritation as he reclined on a lavish chair. "What happened with Lorna? You made sure to get rid of her, I trust?"

"Who cares about that useless child?!" responded Rowser. "It's the mana vein! The great mana vein in the forbidden clearing of the Ipple Woods—it's...it's gone!"

"Wh-what?!" Brau dropped his wine glass in shock. It fell to the ground, shattering into countless pieces. Wine splashed across the expensive carpet at his feet, but he hardly noticed—his attention was now fully devoted to the matter at hand. "You can't be serious!"

"I'm afraid I am... The mana siphons around the vein have all ceased operation."

"That cannot be!"

The great mana vein of the Ipple Woods was said to be the largest source of mana in the world.

Mana siphoned from such veins allowed the people of the world to use magic. Humans needed mana to live. Without mana, the crops would wither and the people would be unable to use the magical tools necessary to purify water and keep their fires lit.

The Guugelheit family had sole ownership of the Ipple Woods vein and had profited greatly from it. If what Rowser said was true, then their future wealth had vanished along with the vein.

But we've taken out countless loans expecting to pay them back with profits from the vein, thought Margrave Guugelheit. *Not to mention the scheme we've been working toward. We need mana for that as well... But that's not even the worst of it.* Brau put his head in his hands. *I-if this news makes it to the king, then...*

The Guugelheit family had been granted a right to the vein in return for keeping it safe. Now that it had disappeared, they would be held responsible.

Worse, if the palace launched an investigation, they would surely discover that the margrave had been embezzling mana.

P-perhaps we can cover this up somehow? No. That would be impossible.

There was no way to disguise the fact that the mana vein was gone. It was only a matter of time before people all over the world knew of its disappearance—and the name of the incompetent family that had allowed it to happen.

There were no two ways about it—their family would be ruined. Dark visions of the future plagued the margrave's thoughts.

"Wh-why?! This shouldn't be possible! Why would the mana vein we've been guarding for millennia suddenly disappear?!"

"We're currently investigating the matter, but...it seems highly likely this catastrophe was caused by...human hands."

"What do you mean?"

"...Moments after the mana vein was extinguished, we detected powerful magic being used in the vicinity of the Ipple Woods. Based on the amount of mana expended, it seems the spell used... over ten thousand MP."

"...?! P-preposterous!"

The maximum amount of MP a human could expend was 999. If Rowser was correct and a being who could use such a spell had appeared, they could hardly be considered human. It would be a magic-wielding, living calamity. Such a being hadn't existed since ancient times, when the Demon Lord had walked the land.

"A-at this rate, these earthquakes are certain to ravage the earth."

This problem was bigger than the Guugelheit domain—the whole world was in danger.

"What in blazes has descended upon our lands? What's to become of the world now...?!" Margrave Brau's voice shook, and his body trembled in awe of this unknown foe.

Meanwhile, completely unaware of the calamity that had befallen her former family's domain and of the tremors that were at that very moment rocking the land, Lorna was desperately trying to put out the fires she'd started by shooting ice at them.

"Waaah! Petit Ice! Petit Ice! Petit Ice!!!"

Crack-crickle-crackk!!!

*　*　*

A wave of ice swallowed up the forest until Lorna stood on what looked like a mountainous glacier.

"Oh! Oh no! Oh no, no, no! Wha—what do I do?!"

This was a disaster. Her staff was too powerful. There was no way for Lorna to control its magic. Even her weak starter spells were enough to cause natural disasters.

Sword Plant swarm defeated! You gained 165 EXP!
Evil Treant swarm defeated! You gained 420 EXP!
LEVEL UP! Lv. 14 ➜ Lv. 15
Paraflower swarm defeated! You gained 220 EXP!
Forest Wolf swarm defeated! You gained 318 EXP!
LEVEL UP! Lv. 15 ➜ Lv. 16
Great Bear defeated! You gained 950 EXP!
LEVEL UP! Lv. 16 ➜ Lv. 17
SKILL UP! Magic III ➜ Magic V
You learned the Petit Heal, Petit Cleanse, and Petit Wall starter spells!

You learned the Art of Slaughter I skill!

"Whyyyyyy?!"

With each spell, Lorna seemed to be slaughtering countless monsters. The level-up sound effect chimed on ceaselessly.

If someone sees me doing this, who knows what might happen...

Lorna imagined it for a second. It wasn't good.

"Gya-ha-ha! Burn the witch!"

"Nooooo!"

Visions of being burned at the stake filled Lorna's imagination. She turned deathly pale.

Not that anyone could hope to take her on now. She could easily drive off any foe. But that fact didn't occur to Lorna, who had until mere moments ago been only Level 1.

"A-anyway. I gotta get out of here, or else... Urgh, why is all this happening?" whined Lorna, tears welling up in her eyes. "All I want is to live a life of freedom."

She quickly looked at the map on the internet and set off in the direction of the nearest town.

Chapter 3 I Tried Taking on the Lord of the Woods!

"Okay! Not much farther until the next town!"

The day after getting the Staff of World Tree and spending the night in the woods, Lorna began making her way to the next town, one eye on the map she'd found on the internet.

The woods had no real path, and it was hard to know which way to go. But thanks to the map, Lorna knew there was a town nearby. And that wasn't all…

"The gathering point on the map *should* be around here som— Oh! Found it!"

Lorna spotted an area to gather medicinal herbs right where the internet had said it would be.

■ **Item: Phantom Leaf**
Type: Material
Price: 50,000 shil
Effect: None
◇ **Details:** A rare medicinal herb from the Magic Forest that grows in very small quantities.
Can be used as a material in high-grade healing items such as Elixirs and Elven Nostrum. Also used as an event item in the side quest, *The Toxic Ambitions of Dr. Zariché*.

* * *

"Yep, it's exactly like the internet said it would be. But wait, hold on a sec. This stuff sells for fifty thousand shil? It says it's super rare, but it just looks like a worthless plant to me…"

Regardless, Lorna stuffed as many of the leaves into her bag as she could every time she passed a gathering point.

"Let's see… It says some goblins made a pitfall trap around here… Is that it?"

She could see that some leaves were piled up in a particularly strange way along the path. If she had been walking by and hadn't known, she never would have noticed it.

"And it looks like there are three Level 4 brown goblins hiding in the grass nearby…"

Lorna pointed her staff at the grass in question.

She guessed that the goblins were hoping to pounce on whoever fell into their trap. But that was nothing to Lorna—she could see through their ruse with the help of the internet.

"Okay, let's start with—Terra Drain!"

This was the skill granted to her when she equipped her SSS-Rank staff, the Staff of World Tree. It allowed her to absorb the MP of all enemies within range.

A massive magic circle shone on the ground underneath Lorna's feet.

"Gyah?!" came the perplexed cries of the goblins.

At the same moment, light began flowing into the green gem at the tip of Lorna's staff.

According to the internet, once a monster's MP was reduced to zero, it would become incapable of performing any actions for a set time.

Lorna took advantage of the opening.

"Brown goblins are weak to wind! So…Petit Gale!"

Lorna used the MP she'd just absorbed to cast one of the spells she'd learned the day before.

Fwooooooosh!!!

A massive tornado appeared that sucked up all the goblins—and the nearby trees along with them.

After a few moments, goblin gems and a host of other materials came falling from the sky.

**Brown Goblin swarm defeated! You gained 108 EXP!
LEVEL UP! Lv. 17 ➜ Lv. 18**

"...Th-this thing is *way* too strong," Lorna muttered as she broke out in a cold sweat.

She was glad she was able to use magic so effectively, but...

"I don't really *need* my spells to do this much damage..."

She had only cast starter spells so far, but based on the outcome, she might as well have been using ultimate magic.

I probably shouldn't use any spells in town if they're all going to do... this.

Lorna looked back over her shoulder.

She could see sharp rocks jutting up toward the sky alongside a mountainous glacier. Nearby, a scorched field still seethed with red-hot embers and a tornado raged, tossing whole trees hither and thither. It looked like the world was ending right behind her.

All she had done was test out a few of her spells. But her staff was way too powerful. It was like the weapon had a mind of its own and was determining the strength of her spells without her input.

"And to think, I got this staff just by following the instructions on the screen... The internet really *is* amazing."

But that wasn't the only thing amazing about it.

"It even has info on how to learn new skills and the weak points of monsters. *No one* knows that kind of stuff."

Those two pieces of knowledge alone were revolutionary.

Lorna popped open the internet and looked up the details of the skills she had learned the day before.

■ **Skill: Giant Killer**

Effect: Boosts damage done to higher-level enemies based on the difference between your levels (difference in level x1 percent)

How to Learn: Solo an enemy twenty levels higher than the character.

How to Enhance: Solo an enemy twenty levels higher than the character.

■ **Skill: Art of Slaughter I**

Effect: Increases damage dealt and critical rate when facing five or more enemies.

How to Learn: Overkill twenty or more enemies within one hour without being attacked.

How to Enhance: Overkill thirty or more enemies while Art of Slaughter I is active.

This is, like, way, way beyond the level of a national secret...

In this world, the skills one was born with (what the internet referred to as the skill gacha) were highly valued. But that was because no one knew what the conditions were for learning or enhancing skills.

Common sense dictated that if you trained hard, you would one day be able to get a skill falling somewhere between G-Rank and E-Rank. If there was a known way to train that would allow someone to obtain a D- or C-Rank skill, that knowledge would be considered a national secret or an esoteric mystery handed down only to chosen successors.

But the internet listed the conditions for learning and enhancing *all* skills—even those of B- and A-Rank.

How's a person supposed to figure out any of this stuff without looking it up on the internet anyway...?

It was the same for monsters' weaknesses. Some were relatively straightforward and easy to figure out—the fact that plant-type monsters were weak to fire, for example. But something like brown goblins being weak to wind made no sense. Surely the only way to know would be to look it up. And knowledge like that was far too valuable to be made publicly available.

Boy, I'd really love to learn some more skills, Lorna thought as she walked through the forest.

Using Terra Drain a few moments ago had really gotten her blood pumping. New skills were always cause for excitement.

"Okay. I should be coming up on the exit soon... But first, I've got one last job to do."

Lorna stopped and her expression grew stern.

At that very moment...

Clomp, clomp, clomp...!

With that sound, a massive boar appeared, knocking over trees as it trundled along. It blocked Lorna's path.

The creature stared her down, letting out an imposing growl and exhaling a plume of white breath before slamming its front hooves into the ground in an attempt to intimidate its foe.

...It's just like the internet said!

The gargantuan boar was the boss of this area—the lord of the Ipple Woods.

■ **Boss: Lord of the Woods**
Spawn Location: Ipple Woods
Level: 50
Weaknesses: Fire, Ice. Weak points in the nose and stomach.
Resistances: Wind, Earth, Poison, Slash

Rewards: Opens main road out of Ipple Woods. Drops Lord of the Woods Gem (90 percent), Lord Pelt (70 percent), Lord Tusk (30 percent), Reckless Boots (20 percent), Chargefang Lance (3 percent)

◇ Details: The area boss of Ipple Woods
Appears to block the exit when you try to leave the woods.
Despite its very simple attack pattern, its high ATK, DEF, and SPD make it practically impossible to defeat early on in the game.
The Lord of the Woods destroys trees and rocks when it charges, so hiding behind rocks or climbing trees is certain to get you hurt.

...This thing looks so much scarier up close.
But Lorna already knew everything she needed to about the beast thanks to the internet.
I just have to believe in the internet. As long as I believe, everything will turn out fine! After all, everything on the internet is tru—

"Groooooorgh!"

"Whaaaa—?!"
Thmp, thmp, thmp, thmp!!
The frenzied lord charged at her. Its sheer power had her completely overwhelmed. She might have looked everything up ahead of time, but that hadn't made the beast any less terrifying.
"R-right! O-okay! Weak to fire and ice! I don't want to set the whole forest on fire again so—Petit Ice!"
"Gergh?!"
The boss was hit with a powerful blast of ice magic from Lorna's SSS-Rank staff. Even a massive beast like the Lord of the Woods let out a horrified cry as it was swallowed by a wave of ice. But...
"Grrroooorrrg!"

Ka-crk!!!

The boar crashed through the ice and was soon charging at Lorna once more.

Yikes! Maybe I shouldn't have expected this thing to go down with one hit from a starter spell. It is Level 50, after all.

It seemed to have taken quite a bit of damage. However, at this rate, Lorna wouldn't be able to take it down before it reached her.

…But she'd expected as much.

"Then how about this? Petit Wall!"

Lorna raised her staff and swung it in the air, and…

Rumble, rumble, rumble…!!!

…a tremendous wall of stone burst from the ground and rose up in front of the boar.

Lorna had gained access to Petit Wall once her Magic skill rose to Magic V.

Yet despite her efforts, the large boar smashed through the wall as though it were made of twigs.

"Petit Wall! Petit Wall! Petit Wall!"

"Grroooh?!"

Lorna retreated backward, dipping into her abundant MP pool to create wall after wall after wall.

This enraged the boar, who smashed through each of them in turn. But Lorna could tell that the beast was starting to lose steam.

That was part one of Lorna's plan. And she had more up her sleeve.

"…You fell for it."

The instant the massive creature smashed through the final wall…

"Groorrgh?!"

Fssssshhhh!

…it slipped, and its monstrous body tumbled into a hole in the ground.

"Yes! Just like I planned!"

It was the very pitfall trap the goblins had set up to trick passersby. Lorna had created wall after wall not only to keep the Lord of the Woods away from her, but also to lure it to this spot.

"...?! ...!"

The beast fell into the hole headfirst and got stuck. Its hooves waggled in the air helplessly. The sheer weight of the beast's massive body seemed to keep it from climbing out.

It might have been able to avoid such a fate if it had been a little more careful. But the beast had been rampaging around blindly, and the walls had further prevented it from taking in its surroundings. It would have been a difficult fate to avoid.

This is all thanks to the internet.

Lorna popped open the screen and looked it over once again.

■ **Boss: Lord of the Woods**
◇ **Strategy: Its basic pattern of attack is to charge head-on, making pitfalls an effective strategy.**

The boss takes a long time to drag itself out of a hole, so surrounding it with pitfalls is a good way to keep it trapped.

If you change the terrain inside the hole to Puddle, the boss will take damage over time, and you can defeat it easily.

If you don't have the Dig, Rabbit Hole, or Groundbreaker skills, you can use the nearby goblin pitfall instead (it was likely put there to be used during this fight).

Wow, all sorts of helpful stuff is written on the internet, huh? But why is it all so specific? Are the gods just really bored or something...?

It seemed strange to Lorna. But she had bigger fish to fry at the moment. Or in this case, boars to freeze.

"Okey dokey, here goes..."

Lorna pointed her staff at the Lord of the Woods, now stuck in the hole.

"All that's left is to attack it again and again until it goes down. Petit Ice!"

She hit the defenseless beast's weak point—its stomach—with a blast of ice.

"Okay! Next is— Wait. Huh?"

Just as Lorna prepared another spell, something happened.

Poof!

The boss's body vanished in a puff of smoke, leaving behind a gem and a variety of dropped items.

Lord of the Woods defeated! You gained 7,500 EXP!
LEVEL UP! Lv. 18 ➔ Lv. 22
SKILL UP! Giant Killer I ➔ Giant Killer II
Obtained Title: "Lord Slayer"

"U-um... It's...over?"

Lorna stood dumbfounded, her staff still at the ready.

The Lord of the Woods was a monster that struck fear in the hearts of those living near the Ipple Woods. Even the Guugelheit family, with their high-ranking skills, stood no chance against the fearsome beast.

And yet Lorna had defeated it with ease. The battle was almost *too* anticlimactic.

Does this mean I could have just hit it one more time, without doing any of that other stuff?

The wide gap between their levels had made Lorna overly cautious, and she'd felt the need to rely on the trap.

But now that she thought about it, she had 3,600 M-ATK. In other words, her M-ATK was seven times higher than the kingdom's strongest sorcerer. Not to mention the fact that the Staff of World Tree doubled the damage of her spells at the cost of using up three times more MP. On top of that, her Magic V skill increased the damage output of her spells by an additional 1.3 times.

Furthermore, the thirty-two-level difference between Lorna and the boar meant Giant Killer I added even *more* damage to the equation: 1.32 times more, to be exact. And finally, she had attacked its weak point, which doubled the total damage.

With all those factors combined, Lorna's attacks dealt roughly *seven* times more damage than normal.

"...Right, well," Lorna said with a vacant expression, "I guess that means I'm pretty strong now. So that's neat."

Lorna gave up trying to figure out her total damage halfway through. She figured it was fairly impressive the boar had even survived one attack from her.

"I guess I should check what the boss dropped," she said, snapping back to her senses.

She picked up the beast's gem and its pelt. The pelt was too big to fit into her bag, however, so she cut off a smaller portion. She assumed that would be more than enough to sell for her travel expenses.

But she found something else, too.

"H-huh. The boss dropped some finished footwear," she said, pulling a pair of boots out of the pitfall. She assumed they were leather shoes made from the pelt of the Lord of the Woods.

Uh... Why are these boots premade? This doesn't make sense. Who made them?

Lorna was confused, but she decided to put those thoughts aside and look up the boots on the internet.

■ **Equipment (Feet): Reckless Boots**
Rank: B
Type: Boots
Price: 5,000,000 shil
Effect: DEF +80, SPD +300
  ◇ **Equip Skill: Reckless Rush (B)**

Effect: Doubles speed, but stopping is impossible for the skill's duration

◇ **Details: Boots dropped by the Lord of the Woods**

The equip skill for these boots comes in handy when traversing the world or escaping, and they remain useful even after their stats get outclassed by other boots.

Activating the skill makes it very hard to control which direction you're going, so be careful not to speed off the side of a cliff and die.

"Wow, these are some strong boots..."

It was hard for Lorna to fathom just how fast SPD +300 was.

Until yesterday, I only had 6 SPD, so...

After getting her SSS-Rank staff, Lorna was becoming desensitized to the ease with which she was earning high-ranked gear. Regardless, she was grateful to have a replacement for her old boots, which had become tattered from her long trip through the woods.

Lorna wasted no time slipping into her new Reckless Boots.

"All right! Not a bad find! ♪"

Nothing could beat the feeling of getting one's hands on some strong new gear.

Lorna hummed a happy tune as she checked the internet once more.

"Let's see... It says the equip skill for the Reckless Boots is called Reckless Rush. Wow, double speed?"

Sure, there was a drawback: Stopping was impossible for the skill's duration. But that didn't seem so bad to Lorna. And besides...

"Apparently, it's an incredibly useful skill. If the internet says so, it must be true."

When she thought of that, Lorna began itching to use it right away. Sure, trying the skill *after* she left the woods would be the safer bet, but why let that stop her?

H–hey, I mean, I just got this skill. I should test it out, shouldn't I?

Lorna couldn't resist the allure of a brand-new skill. And so...

"Okay! Here! We! Go! Reckless Russssssh...?!"

Lorna nonchalantly called out the skill's name. And the very next moment...
FSSSSH!
...Lorna's body was sent hurtling forward.

Or more accurately, her legs seemed to be moving of their own volition, forcing her to run forward at an unfathomable speed.

Taka-taka-taka-taka-taka-taka!!!

The sound of Lorna's recklessly rushed footsteps echoed among the trees as she ran through the woods, kicking up a cloud of dust all the way.

"Fa-fa-fa-fast! Too faaast!!! Whyyyyyyyyy?!"

Lorna had made another miscalculation when she read that the skill would make her run twice as fast. She had forgotten that, between her recent level grinding and her new equipment, she had leapfrogged from 6 SPD to 346 SPD in a matter of hours.

The boost to her stats meant that even a regular run would have been more than fast enough. And now that pace had been doubled.

"Ahhhhhh!!! I'm going to run into a treeeeee! S-s-s-stooooop!" Lorna screamed, tears welling up in her eyes.

She had no idea how to disengage her new skill.

And so she continued running through the forest at top speed, until suddenly...

"I'm...I'm oooout!"

* * *

...the dark thicket of trees gave way, and the scenery ahead opened up.

Lorna somehow managed to screech to a halt, disengaging her skill with a mighty tumble.

She looked up and was astonished.

"W-wow!"

Grassy plains sprawled out as far as the eye could see. A refreshing breeze was blowing, and the light around the sun formed a gentle halo.

A bit farther in the distance, Lorna could make out a sprawling town.

Chapter 4 I Tried Healing a Person in Distress!

"Um, I think this town is called Aiphoné."

Lorna had finally escaped the Ipple Woods and was now walking through a stretch of grassland toward a town. She pulled out the internet to look up some info on the place she was headed.

■ Map: Town of Aiphoné

A town for beginners in the western region of the Kingdom of Ohline.

Depending on the lineage you've chosen, this could be your starting town.

A perfect place for people at the outset. The nearby levels and dungeons (such as the Ipple Woods, the Aios Plains, and the Twilight Temple) are particularly beginner-friendly.

The Guugelheit family has a lot of influence in the town, so many of the side quests found here relate to them in some way.

Its regional delicacies are Ipple pie and Ipple juice.

"...Lineage I've picked? Starting town? Side quests?"

Lorna, as always, didn't understand half of what she was reading.

"Urgh... So the Guugelheit family has a lot of influence here, huh...?"

Lorna's eyes came to rest on that sentence.

There wasn't much for it; she was still within the Guugelheit domain, after all. She wanted to fill her coffers with enough money to fund her travels and get out of her ex-family's domain as soon as possible.

"First things first. The entrance to the town should be…over that way," she said, following the map as she made her way toward the town gates.

"…Ah! You there! Did you perhaps come from the Ipple Woods?" a guard asked her with concern.

He was youthful, with blond hair, and wore his helmet low so it hid his eyes. He held a spear with a blade that zigzagged like a bolt of lightning.

"I'm surprised you were able to make it out! Are you all right? You've not sustained any injuries, have you?"

"…Huh? Did something happen?"

"I would certainly say so! All manner of natural disasters have been ravaging that forest since yesterday. It's caused quite a stir among the townspeople!"

"……"

Lorna turned around silently.

The "natural disasters" that had occurred in the Ipple Woods could be seen from town as clear as day. There was the mountain of ice poking out through the treetops, the jagged fangs of rock, and the massive tornado that continued to rage. All of them were Lorna's doing, of course.

"I—I…uh, I didn't do anything! I'm innocent, I swear!"

"Pardon?"

"U-um, well… Eh-heh-heh… What I meant to say was, wow! That really is something! I hadn't even noticed. How scary!"

Lorna broke out in a cold sweat as she tried to play it cool; her words were stiff and wooden. Of course, despite how suspicious she was acting, the guard would never suspect that the disaster affecting the woods could possibly be the work of the meek young girl before him.

"In any event, I'm glad you've made it to town safely. Now then," he continued, "do you have some form of identification on you?"

"Um... Identification? Am I not allowed to enter town without it?"

"No, no. Nothing quite so severe. Though a lack of identification *will* mean dealing with a rather vexing amount of paperwork." Having said that, the guard held a stone tablet out to her. "How about we start by having you place your hand on this tablet? I need to make sure you don't have a criminal record or anything. For the paperwork, you understand."

"Ah. Right."

Lorna did as she was told and gently placed her hand on the stone. A pattern of pale light glowed on the tablet's surface as it displayed her information.

■ Lorna Hermit, Lv. 22
HP: 94/94
MP: 91,710/138
ATK: 384
DEF: 130
M-ATK: 3,693
MIND: 93
SPD: 346
LUCK: 50

Oh... Oh dear...

As it turned out, the stone tablet showed a person's stats. What's more, the numbers displayed factored in the modifiers from one's equipment. By the time Lorna noticed, it was already too late. There was no way for her to hide it now.

"Hmm, Lorna Hermit, is it? And you're...Level twenty-two?! A-at such a young age! Usually people of that level are veteran adventur— Er, what?! Ninety thousand MP?! Three thousand six hundred and ninety-three M-ATK?!" The guard's face dropped in slack-jawed disbelief.

Uh-oh...

Here was a girl with absurd stats, wandering in from the direction of a series of bona fide natural disasters. To them, she'd surely look like another Demon Lord!

"O-oh gosh! That stone must be broken! I'm just your average, everyday adventurer, you see..."

"Um, y-yes. That must be it. Goodness, what a shock... Anyone with stats like these could hardly be considered human."

"Hah! Ah-ha-ha! Not human, huh? I guess you're right..."

"...?"

Luckily for Lorna, the numbers had been so absurdly high that the guard hadn't suspected her. Even though her incomprehensibly high stats *had* been responsible for the natural disasters.

"Well, in any case, I can see that you have no criminal record... You're welcome to pass, once you've paid the town tax—two hundred shil."

"No problem."

Lorna felt the tension leave her body as she realized she'd talked her way out of the situation. Next time she ran into an inspection like this, she'd have to unequip everything *beforehand*. Just as she was pondering that...

"Tell me—do you intend to embark on a journey?" asked the guard.

"...Oh? Um, yes. That was the plan anyway."

"In that case, you would do well to join the Adventurers Guild."

"You mean I should become an adventurer? But don't you have to be a big muscly muscleman for that?"

"Ha-ha... I think you may have confused rumors with reality. The truth is: There are many adventurers in this day and age. And a number of them are young ladies such as yourself. In any event, if you join the guild, you'll be given an Adventurer Card that can act as your identification. I suggest you think it over. They also offer work if you're low on money."

"Oh, huh. I had no idea."

"Indeed. And best of all, it makes it far easier to pay your taxes. One of the trickiest things about being a traveler is how to handle all your tax payments. But if you join the guild, they take a portion of your earnings and allocate it toward taxes for you. That way, you don't have to worry about the individual tax systems for every town you visit. And there's no risk of being arrested for tax evasion. I would say it's well worth the effort of joining."

"T-taxes, huh...? I hadn't even thought of those."

Only two days prior, Lorna had been a noble. She had hardly ever left her estate. Naturally, she'd been ignorant of such things.

She assumed the best course of action was to take the guard's advice and join the guild.

"Well, in that case...I suppose I'll go and pay this Adventurers Guild a visit."

"A splendid idea," said the guard with a contented smile.

The kindly young man continued talking, filling Lorna in on more details about the guild. There was something in the way he spoke about adventurers that made it sound like he really admired them.

"You certainly know a lot about adventurers, huh?" Lorna said.

"Hmm? Ah, I suppose so... In truth, I used to be one. But then I took an arrow in the knee..."

The youthful guard grimaced as he rubbed his leg. Lorna *had* noticed that he was leaning heavily on his spear. But more than that...

"An arrow in the knee, you say...?"

Something about those words rang a bell. In fact, Lorna was looking at them right now on the internet.

■ **Side quest: Soldier Who Took an Arrow in the Knee**
Recommended Level: 20
Activation Conditions: Adventurer rank is bronze or higher
Location: Entrance to Aiphoné
Reward: Bolt Spear
◇ Details: "The First Guard," Reinharte the guardsman's side quest
Reinharte is looking for the phantom hot spring in order to treat his knee. Accompany him through the Ipple Woods and keep him safe. While the recommended level is a bit high, doing this side quest is well worth the effort, as the spear you're rewarded with comes in very handy at the port town of Aquas.

"Oh dear... I can't believe it even knows private information about people."

"...Hmm? Is something the matter? What are you looking at...?"

"Oh! Uh, nothing!" said Lorna, playing dumb.

It was hard for her to pretend she knew nothing when she was in possession of such intimate details about the guard's personal woes.

Actually...didn't I just learn a new healing spell? I don't know if it'll work, but...he's helped me out a lot, so...

After thinking it over for a moment, Lorna pointed her staff at the guard.

"Petit Heal!"

* * *

The instant she called out the name of her spell, the heavens parted and a brilliant light shone down on the area. It was as though the gods themselves were blessing the land.

Uh... What's this crazy atmosphere?

She'd only used the weakest beginner heal spell. She figured this was, once again, the doing of her SSS-Rank staff. Maybe it had fully healed the guard. She hoped that if it hadn't, it had at least granted him some relief.

"Wh-what is—?"

"Oh, well, you know... You just helped me out so much. So I cast a little healing spell. I hope your knee gets better, Mr. Reinharte."

"...Um, thank...you?" he responded, cocking his head in confusion.

"Anyway! I'll be heading into town now, if that's all right."

"Ah yes. In that case..."

The guard smiled and opened his arms wide.

"...allow me to officially welcome you to the town of Aiphoné."

Lorna walked through the entrance, and Reinharte watched as she disappeared into the distance.

"Hold on...," he said, suddenly confused. "That girl... How did she know my name?"

A little while after their meeting, Reinharte found himself thinking idly about the girl he'd just met.

What a strange young lady she was.

Something about her had felt almost otherworldly.

Because the stone tablet had malfunctioned, he didn't know what her real stats looked like, but he knew she must have an impressive amount of natural talent to be able to reach Level 22 at her age.

I'm rather envious. A girl like that, why, she can go anywhere she likes.

Reinharte leaned his body weight on his spear and stared absentmindedly out at the expanse of grassy meadows before him.

It had already been five years since he quit adventuring and became a guard. Up to that point, he'd spent his life believing he was a natural-born adventurer.

Reinharte Highwind, the Swift. User of the B-Rank skill, Lightning Spear.

Despite his young age, he rose through the ranks to become a gold-ranked adventurer, and his feats earned him some renown in the region. But perhaps it was the same youthful recklessness that had served him so well that ultimately led to his downfall.

After taking an arrow from a dungeon trap in the knee, he was forced to retire from adventuring. His comrades abandoned him, and he forever lost the swiftness of foot that had gained him such fame.

Despite his struggles, he hoped to one day find a way to mend his knee and resume his adventures. In the meantime, he settled on serving as a guard at the town gate in the hopes that, if nothing else, he could keep gazing at the outside world he loved so dearly.

But slowly, without him even noticing it, something inside him changed.

His eyes no longer took in the scenery of the outside world. His ears no longer pricked up at travelers' tales of adventure. The breeze that blew in from across the boundless plains no longer stirred his spirit.

Somewhere along the way, their charms had faded for him. Now all they did was make his injured knee ache.

So he once more pulled his helmet down low over his eyes, hoping to shut out the outside world.

And just as he did…

"Heeey, Reiny. 'Bout time for your lunch break, eh?"

…a middle-aged, senior guard called out to him.

"I'm not a kid, you know. It's about time you stopped calling me Reiny, Wol."

"How 'bout you get yourself a lady friend before you start pretendin' to be an adult."

"Ha-ha... Very funny. I suppose when you put it that way, there's not much room for retort." Reinharte tried to play off Wol's teasing with a wry smile. The fact that he still yearned for adventure made starting a family difficult. "Oh, right... The stats tablet seems to be acting up. It might be broken."

"Yeah? Prob'ly just its time. 'Course, I bet you could fix the thing if you gave it a few good whacks."

"Ha-ha... Maybe so. In any case, I'll take my lunch now."

With that, Reinharte began to walk away. But as he did, he noticed something strange...

".........What?"

His knee. It no longer hurt.

Usually, every step he took would make his knee creak in pain.

"It...can't be."

The spear he used as a walking stick fell from his hand. And somehow, he could still stand. The wind blew, yet his knee didn't hurt.

Even the former physician to the imperial court had been unable to do anything to mend his knee. And yet here it was, completely healed.

"Wh-why...?"

And just as Reinharte was coming to terms with his bewildering good fortune...

"Huh? Hey, Reiny! Ain't nothin' wrong with this stats tablet."

".........Pardon?"

...his fellow guardsman's words struck the finishing blow to his psyche.

The stats tablet...isn't broken? But that would mean the girl's stats were accurate...

If that was true, then...

"I hope your knee gets better, Mr. Reinharte."

That strange girl—she had cast a healing spell on him, hadn't she? Could she have fixed his knee? That was the only possibility.

"J-just who was that girl...? Who—or what—did I just let into town?"

There was so much he didn't understand.

Asking for neither payment nor praise, she had performed a miracle healing on him and then disappeared. It was like he had met some angelic being from a fairy tale.

But regardless of how it had happened, one thing was clear—his knee was healed. And that meant only one thing.

"...!"

In a single movement that released years of pent-up frustrations, Reinharte pulled his helmet off and threw it to the ground. Then he raised his face and looked out at the expanse before him.

Oh... I had almost forgotten.

He finally recalled just how wide and vast the world truly was. He remembered how pleasant the gentle breeze felt as it blew across the plains.

He felt it in his bones—the world sprawling out before him was his to explore.

But that wasn't all. There was more, so much more. He could go farther still, across the boundless horizon.

"......"

All it would take would be one step, and then another.

Reinharte began to walk on uneasy legs toward the horizon... Then he fell to his knees. Tears were streaming down his face.

"Wh-whoa! You all right, Reiny? Your knee actin' up again?"

"No, I'm just... I'm just so happy..."

But was it too late? His leg muscles had atrophied from years of disuse. No doubt, he would need rehabilitation. His combat instincts had likely dulled with time as well. And yet...

"Can I...can I really become an adventurer again?" he muttered, eyes ever on the horizon.

Meanwhile, Lorna was making her way through town without the slightest inkling of the human drama she had left in her wake.

"Heh...heh-heh-heh... So this town is known for Ipple pie, huh...? Mmmmm..."

Chapter 5 I Tried Taking the Adventurers Exam!

"Wow! It's a real-life town!"

Lorna had finally arrived safely at her destination—the town of Aiphoné. Her eyes sparkled with excitement as she took in the sights. She'd spent most of her life confined to her family's estate, and this was her first time seeing such a place.

The streets bustled with the comings and goings of people. Colorful stalls lined the avenues like little jewelry boxes. On second thought, maybe things were a little *too* bustling...

"Gaaaaah! A calamity's befallen the Ipple Woods!"
"This town is done for!"
"We've gotta get outta here!!!"

Surely this wasn't normal...

"It's the Demon Lord! The Demon Lord is back! We're done for! It's the end of the world!"
"Just what are those Guugelheit fat cats thinking?! They're always bossing us around! Now look what they've done to us!"
"Waaaaah! Mommyyy! Help meee!"

"............Huh."

Lorna looked out into the distance.

It's a bit different than I expected...

It seemed the spells Lorna cast in the woods were causing quite a panic in town. She kept walking, pretending she didn't see anything. But then...

"Ngh..."

Gurgle...

The sweet smell wafting from a nearby street stall made Lorna's stomach grumble.

Come to think of it, I haven't eaten much of anything since I got kicked out...

She'd only munched on a couple of Ipple fruits she found at spots the internet had labeled gathering points.

Lorna staggered toward the food stall, drawn in by the delicious scent.

"P-pardon me... One Ipple pie, please."

"Huh? Oh, uh, right. You're surprisingly calm right now, young lady."

"Well, y'know, I've gotten used to it."

"...?"

The stall owner looked perplexed as he handed her the pie.

According to the internet, this dish was the town's local delicacy.

■ **Item: Ipple Pie**
Type: Cooking
Price: 200 shil
Effect: Restores HP/MP by 10 (cannot be used in battle)
◇ **Details:** Aiphoné's local specialty. Despite its cheap price of 200 shil, it restores a set amount of MP. This makes it an invaluable item early on in the game.

"This...this is the first time I've ever bought food for myself."

Lorna gulped. Then, resolving herself, she took a big bite of the pie.

"Yum, it's very—HHHHOT?!"

The moment her teeth crunched through the pie crust, Lorna felt a scalding gush of fruity goodness hit the inside of her mouth. She was unaccustomed to biting into piping hot pies, and she could feel her mouth burning.

"Ho-hot...! Hot! Bu'... Goo'! It'sh sho goo'! Mmm."

The crust was nice and crispy, and the filling had a full-bodied sweet taste balanced with a hint of refreshing sourness. The aroma of butter and cinnamon tickled Lorna's nostrils ever so slightly.

Now that she had bought the pie, Lorna had only one hundred shil to her name. But she didn't regret her purchase for a second.

"...I love adventuring," she said, satisfied.

Back home, she'd only been allowed to eat so-called delicacies (basically, fancy junk that looked pretty but tasted horrible). On top of that, the atmosphere at the dinner table was always so intense that it was hard to enjoy one's food.

"I looove being freeee! ♪"

Lorna was once again grateful for her expulsion from the Guugelheit family.

As she finished off her Ipple pie, she wandered around and looked at some nearby stalls.

Whoa, the most basic potion costs two thousand shil. Even a bundle of herbs is four hundred... And some preserves are one thousand? Oh man... Look at the armor. A decent piece'll set you back a whopping one hundred thousand.

Everything she looked at was completely out of her price range. And according to the internet, these prices were on the *cheap* side.

She'd been hoping to get out of the Guugelheit domain as quickly as possible, but...

It looks like preparing for an adventure, even just getting the basics, is

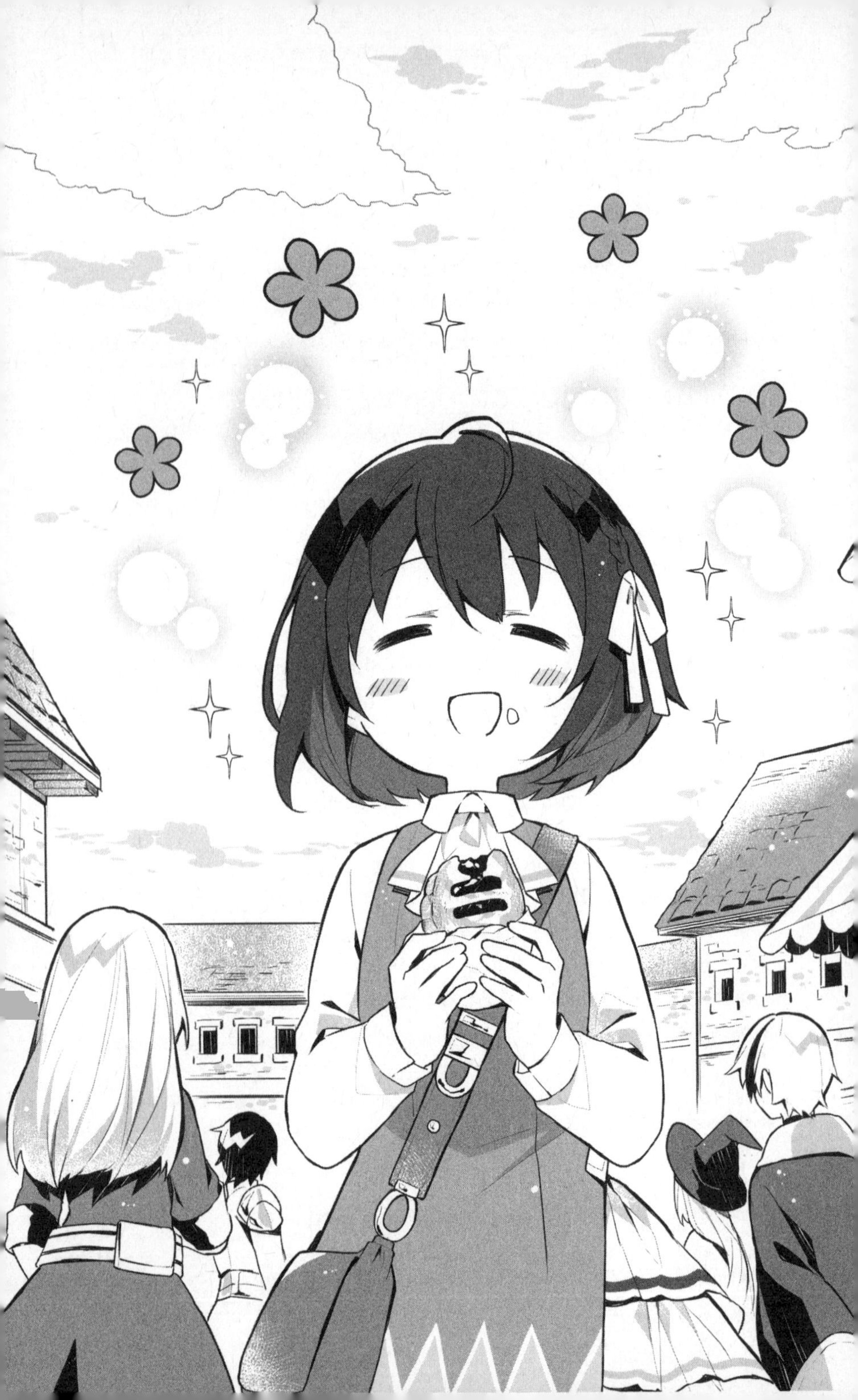

going to set me back at least thirty thousand shil. And if I want to get out of the Guugelheit domain, I'll need at least one hundred thousand... I can't believe how much adventuring costs.

Regardless of what she did next, Lorna was going to need more money. And considering the hubbub around town surrounding the natural disasters, she thought it would draw too much attention to sell the stuff she'd collected in the woods... Besides, she wasn't confident that what she had on hand would net her enough money anyway.

There has to be some way for me to get my hands on some shil...

Lorna immediately started searching the internet for ways to make money.

"Um, forex...? Virtual currency? Gamble online? What is all this? Oh! 'Congratulations, you've been selected by lottery to win a fabulous prize!' ...What?! I've never won anything before! So I just have to tap this button and I get the money?!"

Apparently, unbeknownst to Lorna, the world was full of ways to make money.

"Wow, look at this one. It says that even if you don't have a skill, you can make one million a month with a side job! All I have to do is buy these cheap teaching materials! That sounds like a real bargain!"

Lorna pushed the APPLY NOW button as soon as she spotted it.

This kept up for a while. Lorna was completely absorbed by the joys of the internet. Until...

"...Huh?"

...she suddenly snapped back to her senses. She'd finally realized how much time had passed. She looked around in a panic and saw that everyone was staring at her suspiciously.

Uh-oh. Looks like it's pretty easy to lose track of time when I'm looking at the internet... I should probably be more careful when there are people around.

Lorna, her face now flushed with embarrassment, rushed off. Once she was clear of the area, she pulled herself together.

Anyway, I should probably see how much I can get for what I have. I need money if I want to sleep indoors tonight.

Right now, she didn't even have enough to stay at the cheapest of inns. But before any of that, she figured she ought to start by registering as an adventurer.

But if I want to register, I have to take a test, don't I? Urgh... I hope I can handle it...

The thought made her anxious. But without much choice, Lorna headed for the Adventurers Guild headquarters.

Around the time Lorna was filling out the paperwork to take the adventurers exam, a certain exchange was taking place at the guild's training hall.

A teenage girl walked over to the middle-aged examiner. The young woman was dressed like a witch, and her hair trailed down her back like a red shock of flames. She flashed the examiner a piercing look.

"Um, ex*cuse* me. You're in my way."

"P-pardon me...! I-if it isn't Lady Elmina!"

The moment the examiner realized who he was dealing with, he fell to his knees in apology. His reaction made perfect sense, of course, for the girl in question was none other than...

...Elmina Manaflame, the Witch of Conflagration.

Elmina was a prodigious witch who had manifested the A-Rank skill, Inferno Magic. She was also the master of the Adventurers Guild, and all at the young age of nineteen.

But even more importantly, she was a personal mage of the Guugelheit family, who governed this domain.

"To what do we owe the pleasure, Guild Mistress? I was under the impression that you were out investigating the recent natural disasters..."

"Hmph. That should be obvious. I, an elite among elites, the Witch of Conflagration, Mistress Elmina Manaflame, am here to serve as special examiner!"

"B-but...Mistress Elmina! Every time you proctor an examination, all the participants fail. And that's not to mention the countless injuries—"

"*Excuse* me? Is that whining I hear? I'll have you know that this is a direct mandate from the Guugelheit family. Or are you saying you wish to defy me, an elite among elites and the Guugelheits' personal mage?"

"N-no, I..."

Elmina haughtily pointed at the badge on her chest. It was emblazoned with the seal of the Guugelheit family. "I'm only going to tell you this once: There's no room in this guild for people who irk me."

"I—I beg your pardon...!" the examiner said, bowing his head low.

In the town of Aiphoné, the power of the Guugelheit family was absolute. They'd placed their agents in charge of the town's various industries, and no one dared stand up to them.

"Anyway...I hear there's a girl taking the exam today," Elmina said. "Lorna Hermit. Ring any bells?"

"Oh, um, yes," replied the examiner. "I believe I recall seeing that name on the—"

"Fail her."

"...Pardon?"

"And make her suffer. Enough that she never wants to try again. Got it? That's an order from above."

"B-but why?"

"This is a direct command from the House of Guugelheit. Is that not reason enough?"

"...Oh! V-very well, Mistress Elmina."

In truth, Elmina didn't know many details herself. The night before, she had received the following message from her employers via a communications crystal: *"If a girl named Lorna Hermit shows up, make her suffer. And then fail her."*

Though they hadn't given her an explanation, Elmina had an idea of what this was about.

I recall the Guugelheits had a girl of about fifteen years old named Lorna, and they mentioned this Hermit girl was a nobody with a worthless skill... She probably manifested some useless trash skill and got kicked out. Oh, it must be so dreadful not to be an elite.

Strength was everything in this world. That was why no one could stand up to the Guugelheit family, and why that same family had no issues expelling a weak daughter at the drop of a hat.

But if you were powerful, you were entitled to anything you wanted.

Oh, what a perfect world. If you're me, that is. ♪

Elmina gracefully took a seat, raised a wine glass, and began to swish around the liquid inside.

Those like Elmina, who possessed an A-Rank skill, were born with a silver spoon in their mouth and guaranteed easy success in life. Those with D-Rank skills were thought of as quite powerful, and those with C-Rank skills were considered practically superhuman. Naturally, no one could defy Elmina.

The people of her hometown feared her, and she was the undisputed top of her class at the Institute of Magic. By the simple grace of possessing an A-rank skill, she was able to become retainer to the Guugelheit family and take over the Adventurers Guild right after graduation.

Heh-heh-heh... Not that being guild master of some Podunk little town could ever satisfy me.

She had plans to increase her favor with the Guugelheits and, slowly but surely, carve a path for herself to become a wealthy noble. To Elmina Manaflame, the story of her elite rise to power was only just beginning.

"Now, then! Bring out the examinees. Or do you plan on wasting the time of an elite?"

"Y-yes! I mean, no! Right away, Mistress!"

At the guild master's command, the examinees all filed into the training hall.

There certainly are a lot of them this time around, thought Elmina.

For one reason or another, getting rich quick by exploring dungeons seemed to be all the rage. This batch of young people must've caught the bug. That said, they all looked like weaklings.

Sigh. What a chore. Oh well. Mana Scan!

Elmina activated a skill that allowed her to visualize a target's MP. MP was, after all, necessary for all magic and skills. In other words, one could judge a person's strength based on how much MP they had.

Let's see... Fail. Fail. Fail... Look at all these failures. Not a single elite in the bunch.

With one glance, Elmina began to write big X's next to each name on her list.

I don't know which one of these losers is Lorna Hermit, but I don't see anyone here with a high-ranking skill. In fact, I've already grown weary of this rabble. I suppose I'll simply fail them all. Elmina brought her wine glass to her lips and took a sip of Ipple juice.

But just then, she heard a voice from somewhere near the training hall entrance. It seemed someone had shown up late.

"Ohhh geez... I'm so, so nervous..."

The final examinee was a lone girl. She seemed to lack confidence, and her shoulders slumped pathetically. But the instant she entered the training hall...

* * *

Fwooooooooooooooooooosh!!!

A massive aura engulfed everyone present. It seemed large enough to reach the sky. It might as well have turned the other examinees to dust on the spot. The guild master took the full brunt of it head-on.

"……………………………"

Juice dribbled out of Elmina's mouth uncontrollably.
Wh-what is this…thing that's just entered the hall…?
Elmina unconsciously rubbed her eyes in absolute disbelief.
Is…is that…the Demon Lord…?
Elmina took a close look at the young girl. She was staring around vacantly, and quite honestly looked like a complete fool. But the powerful aura she was draped in…

Fwoooooooosh!!!

…stretched skyward like a massive tornado of flames. Elmina was looking at a veritable geyser of mana. It was as though the incarnation of despair itself had come to pay her a visit.
N-no… This can't be… Surely, something's wrong with my Mana Scan. There's no way any human could have that much mana. If she did…it would mean the second coming of the Demon Lord…or something comparable, at least.
Just as Elmina convinced herself of this…

Crrrack!

…the MP-sensing crystal behind her exploded into pieces.
"Oh my. What's happened? Was it damaged?" asked the examiner. "And it was such a useful crystal, too…"

"............................"

"Mistress Elmina? You seem unwell all of a sudden."

Elmina's mouth was agape. She was frozen stiff.

That crystal was theoretically capable of detecting up to 999 MP. But without the girl even touching it, it had shattered.

............This is really happening, huh.

Wait. Wait. Wait, wait, wait. This isn't right. Why haven't I been informed of this?

Why would this monster, whatever it is, come to this town out in the middle of nowhere to take the adventurers exam?

With that much power, she could easily make the whole world her plaything.

"......"

Elmina had a sudden realization.

The girl she had been told to torment and fail was called Lorna Hermit. A fifteen-year-old with black hair.

No, no, no... There's no way she's...Lorna Hermit...is there? That makes no sense. Why would they chase out someone like that...? It can't be. Please tell me it's not her. Please, please, please, it can't be!

"...?"

The black-haired girl noticed Elmina looking at her, almost like she was praying. Taken aback, she bowed her head.

"I'm Lorna Helmet! I mean, Hermit! It's a pleasure to—"

"Ahhhhh!!! This can't beeeee!"

"Wh-wha—?!"

Elmina broke out in a cold sweat all over her body.

No, no, no, no, no, no! This makes no sense! What the hell were they thinking, throwing out a girl this powerful?! What happened to her being a loser with a trash skill?! Are they stupid?! Are they blind?!

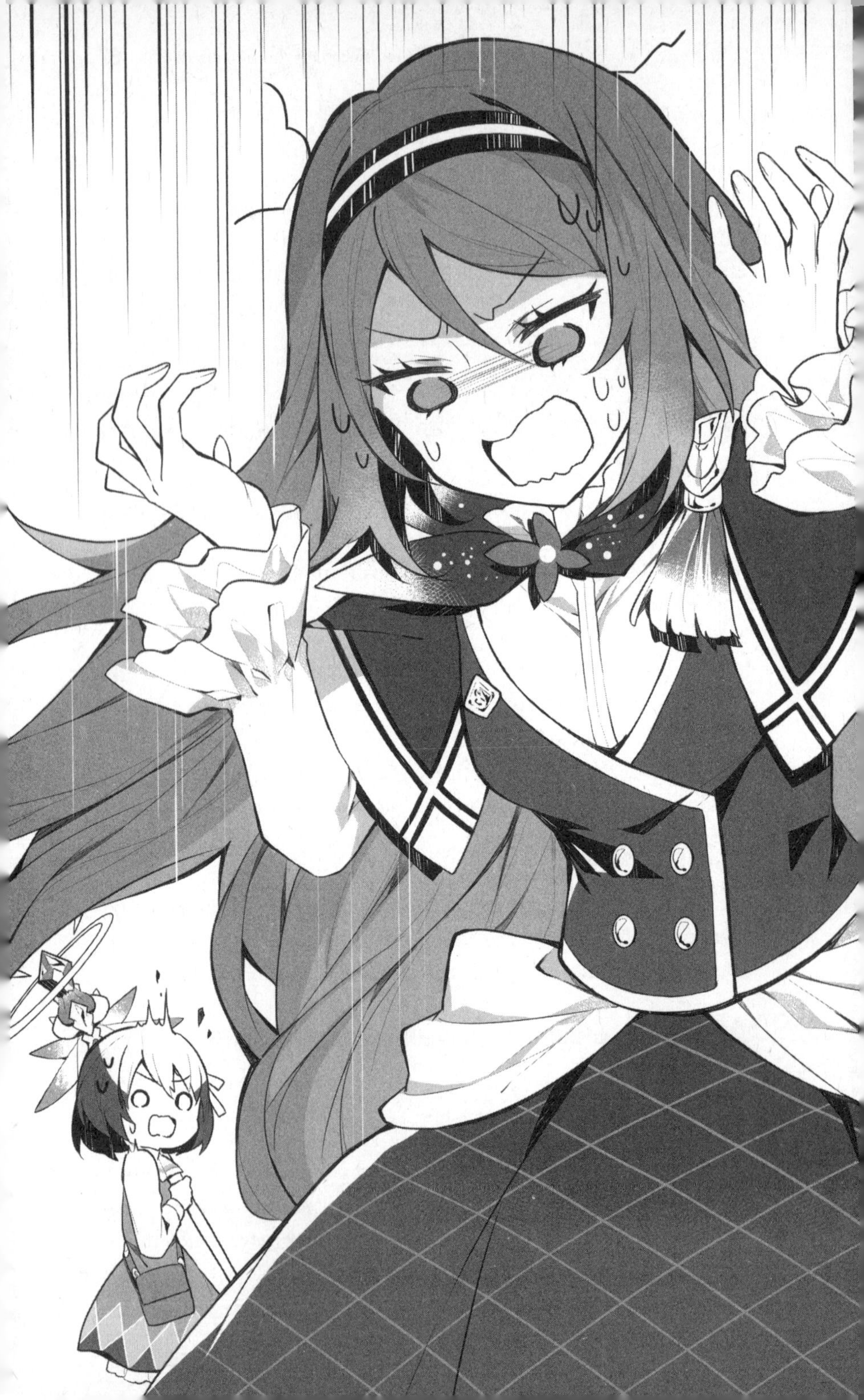

Despite what she had heard about the "nobody with a worthless skill" named Lorna Hermit, it seemed that the real deal was a force to be reckoned with.

If she were to befriend this creature, not even the state itself could stand up to her.

A-are they seriously telling me to fail this Demon Lord–class monster? And I'm supposed to make her suffer enough that she never wants to take the exam again? Um, hello? How in the world am I supposed to do something like that?

If Elmina failed this force of nature for some frivolous reason, she felt certain she'd be erased from existence. *She* was far more likely to wind up suffering.

On the other hand, if she opposed the Guugelheit family's orders, her elite lifestyle would be turned upside down overnight.

What should I do? What can I do?!

Cold sweat poured from Elmina's brow. But before she could reach a conclusion, the middle-aged examiner stepped forward.

"You there, girl. Your name is Lorna, correct? You can forget about the examination. You fail."

""Uh, what?"" Lorna and Elmina responded in unison.

"This woman here is an A-Rank skill bearer—Mistress Elmina Manaflame, the Witch of Conflagration, and there is no room in this guild for people who irk her. In fact, she makes a habit of saying as much to us."

"Wha—? B-but…!" Lorna was stunned. She looked over at Elmina.

Wh-why?! Elmina thought frantically. *Now she's turning her aggro on me, you buffoon! I mean, yes, it's true that I say that constantly. And okay, sure, I did get a bit full of myself and say it literally minutes ago, but still!*

No one in the room noticed Elmina's growing sense of panic. Instead, the other examinees followed the examiner's lead and laughed derisively at Lorna.

* * *

"Heh-heh-heh… Look how spooked she is. She would've failed anyway, I bet."

"Why's a loser like her even trying to become an adventurer?"

"She clearly doesn't know her place. Someone like her doesn't deserve to breathe the same air as we do."

They continued on and on, not understanding the unfathomable gap between Lorna's power and their own. No doubt they hoped to get on Elmina's good side by deriding the latecomer. However…

D-don't tell me… Is everyone here so weak and useless that none of them have noticed how powerful Lorna is?!

Elmina, full of terror, looked over at the girl.

Her face had turned red, and she was trembling. But there was no way someone of her unfathomable strength could be afraid. There was only one possibility—Lorna was shaking with intense rage.

At this rate, she'll kill us all!

"H-hey! All of you! Apologize to Lorna! Right noooow!"

"Wh-whaaaaat?!" The examiner was shocked by Elmina's soulful cry. "But, Mistress Elmina! You said that we were to fail the one called Lorna He—"

"The examination must be just and fair, you fool!!!"

"Whaaaat?!"

Everyone else watched, mouths agape, as Elmina approached Lorna, rubbing her hands together as if trying to appease an angry guest.

"I am so, *so* sorry about that, Miss Lorna. Eh-heh-heh… Please, take a seat on my chair."

"Oh, uh, thank you…I think?" Lorna blinked a few times in confusion. She then noticed something on Elmina's chest and stared for a moment. "Oh! Is that…the Guugelheit crest?"

"...?!"
Lorna's words drew the attention of the other examinees.

"Hey...yeah! That's the badge of a Guugelheit retainer...!"
"I'd heard rumors, but I can't believe she managed it at her age..."
"I'd hate to piss off the Guugelheits... I'd be dead meat..."

The frightened whispers of the examinees filled the training hall. Usually, this would be Elmina's cue to proudly show off her badge.
No...noooo! Sweat poured from Elmina's body. *If Lorna Hermit was banished from the family, then that must mean...she must hate the Guugelheits! Right?!*
Since Elmina was a Guugelheit retainer, Lorna would surely treat her as an enemy.

"Die, retainer scum."

Elmina vividly imagined Lorna's scorn.
"Hmph!" she grunted, tearing the badge off her chest and throwing it as hard as she could to the ground.
"M-Mistress Elmina! What are you—?!"
"Wh-what is this garbage that's mysteriously attached itself to my clothing?!"
"Garbage...? But, Mistress Elmina! That badge is your pride and joy! The symbol that you are a retainer of the Guugelheit family!"
"Oh, I was right...," said Lorna. "So you're one of the Guugelheit—"

"Burn, Guugelheit scum!!!"

Elmina used her Inferno Magic skill to blow the Guugelheit badge to pieces. Everyone present watched in complete disbelief as the badge was reduced to cinders.
"A-are you certain about this, Mistress?"

"......don't......"

"Pardon?"

Elmina fell to her knees on the spot.

"I...don't know... Nothing makes sense anymore..."

"Mistress Elmina?! Are you feeling unwell?!"

As everyone looked at her in concern, Elmina was lost in thought.

Why...? Why did it have to be like this?

As an A-Rank skill bearer, Elmina should have been guaranteed the life of an elite. But if she were to fail Lorna sight unseen, the girl would no doubt kill her. And yet if she *didn't* fail Lorna, the Guugelheits would brand her a traitor. Anyone who betrayed them was certain to meet a horrible fate. It didn't matter which way she leaned—only despair awaited her.

This...this can't be how it ends... I'm supposed to be destined for greatness.

She had no choice. The life of an elite was the only life she knew. She had to figure out some way to make Lorna Hermit fail the examination. And that wasn't all. Lorna needed to fail spectacularly—badly enough that she would never try again.

And in order to make that happen...

...Looks like I've only got one choice.

...Elmina was going to have to risk it all.

If she succeeded, she could seal away this monster named Lorna Hermit for good.

But as she thought it over, Elmina already felt uneasy about her chances. Still, this was her only path forward.

Meanwhile, as Lorna watched Elmina, currently lost in inner turmoil, only one thought came to mind.

This person... She seems really weird...

Chapter 5: I Tried Taking the Adventurers Exam!

Lorna tilted her head in confusion, not realizing that *she* was the cause of the guild master's woes.

At that point, she decided to open the internet in incognito mode so no one else could see what she was doing.

■ **Character: Elmina Manaflame**
Guild master of the Aiphoné Adventurers Guild.
Wielder of the A-Rank skill, Inferno Magic. Also known as the Witch of Conflagration.
Elmina is an elite spellcaster and retainer of the Guugelheit family.
She is very popular in the fandom, especially in a certain section of the fan art community.
MASSIVE SPOILERS BELOW!

So she's a Guugelheit retainer, huh? And yet...
Lorna thought back to Elmina's words a moment prior.
"The examination must be just and fair, you fool!!!"
"Burn, Guugelheit scum!!!"
Elmina's cries had felt like they came straight from the depths of her soul.
She must be a noble-hearted person who doesn't let power go to her head.
And so, unbeknownst to Elmina, Lorna was already warming up to her.

Chapter 6 I Tried Exploring a Dungeon!

"Now, then! This dungeon, the Twilight Temple, is where we will hold the exam."

A short while after Lorna arrived to take the adventurers exam, she and the other examinees were led to the beginner dungeon just outside town by Elmina, the exam's proctor.

"All of you will be exploring this dungeon alone. If you can complete the task written on the piece of paper I handed to each of you, you pass. However, if you use a Wings of Return item to warp back to the dungeon entrance, you will be immediately disqualified. Do keep that in mind."

Each examinee looked at the slip of paper in their hand. Relief seemed to wash over the group.

"Seriously? This is it? Doesn't look like this exam's gonna be so tough," one of them said.

"All we gotta do is go into a beginner dungeon? This is way easier than last time."

"I was worried it was going to be something like a mock battle against an A-Rank skill wielder again…"

Based on everyone's reactions, it seemed like the examination wouldn't be particularly difficult. Feeling relieved, Lorna looked down at the piece of paper she had been given.

* * *

Task: Retrieve the Labyrinth Core from the deepest level of the dungeon

"……………………Hmm?"

That sounded plenty difficult to Lorna.

Do people really think this…is easy?

Lorna wasn't particularly knowledgeable about dungeons, but getting to the bottom level did not sound *easy* to her. However, since Elmina was the examiner, Lorna thought there must be some reason behind the choice. Someone like her would never give out an unreasonably difficult task.

"*The examination must be just and fair, you fool!!!*"

Lorna hadn't sensed so much as an ounce of deceit in that soulful cry. So the obvious conclusion was that everyone had been given a more or less equal trial.

This is a beginner dungeon, right? Maybe it really will be easy, thought Lorna.

"Lorna Hermit… It's your turn."

"Oh! Okay!"

She stepped up when her name was called and took her turn entering the dungeon. Once inside, she carefully descended the stairs into the underground temple.

"Whoa…"

From out of the darkness, a golden structure appeared. Lorna looked up and saw that the cave ceiling was covered with crystallized gems that shone with a bright golden light. They looked like stars and lit the path into the temple.

"It's so pretty," said Lorna, feeling just like a tourist on vacation. "…Oh!"

Then she remembered that this was an examination and quickly snapped back to her senses.

I really need to focus on the exam. Do you think...it would be cheating if I used the internet? She thought this over for a moment. *Yeah... this seems like a bit of a pain. I should just look it up.*

Internet was one of the skills at her disposal, after all. So without further ado, she looked up the dungeon.

■ **Map: The Twilight Temple**
A beginner dungeon west of Aiphoné.
The dungeon was created long ago by the Twilight Dragon Cult. The magic power of the dragon sealed within has, over millennia, crystallized to form gems that line the walls and ceiling of the dungeon.
The temple is primarily used as a tutorial for dungeon puzzles during the starting hours of the main story. But once you have finished part one and obtained the key words, you can get to the bottom floor of the dungeon to fight the boss.

"All right. Looks like there's a map here as well. First, I'd better get to the bottom floor. It's nine levels down, huh? I guess if I can get there, I'll find the Labyrinth Core."

Lorna was a bit nervous. This was her first time in a dungeon. But thankfully, she had the internet on her side.

With its help, she could see the map for every floor all the way to the bottom. She even knew where to expect traps, how to solve the puzzles, and where monsters would spawn. She knew it all. All she had to do was follow along.

"Okay, so... There should be a trap here," said Lorna, as she hopped over a spot on the floor to avoid it. "This chest here is a Mimic, and...it looks like there's an item on the ground in this small room over here."

She searched for a small indentation in the floor and a glittering medal. This was an item called an Ancient Medal. They could be traded to people called Medal Collectors for rare items. Or at least, that was what it said on the internet.

"And it looks like monsters show up right around this corner."

Before proceeding, Lorna tapped her staff against the ground. According to the map, she was just close enough to be in range of the monsters.

"All right—Terra Drain!"

She cast her MP-absorbing area of effect spell.

Gyaaaah!

The monsters cried out, and green-colored light flowed from around the corner and into the jewel adorning Lorna's staff.

She peeked her head around to see the effects of her spell. The bat monsters were incapacitated now that their MP had been reduced to zero. They had fallen to the ground and lay motionless. Lorna pointed her staff toward them.

"Giant Bats are weak to Ice, so... Petit Ice!"

Crack-crickle-crackk!

A wave of ice shot from her staff, freezing the bats, the traps, and the entire hallway along with them.

Giant Bat swarm defeated! You gained 202 EXP!

"All right, looking good! ♪"

Lorna had been a little nervous entering a dungeon for the first time, but it seemed like it wouldn't be so difficult after all.

"Is every dungeon going to be this easy? I feel kind of guilty...," she muttered. She felt bad for all the adventurers of the world who had to struggle their way through dungeons.

The scenery here is so beautiful. It feels like I'm on a nice little hike. It might be pretty fun to play tourist and visit all the dungeons around the world.

Lorna skipped along, humming as she went. It almost felt like this place was designed to be fun. Just walking around it was strangely pleasant.

"It looks like getting to the bottom floor's going to be a piece of cake!"

◇

"...The bottom floor of the dungeon?! Mistress Elmina, did you really give that girl such a dangerous task?"

"Yes... I did."

Meanwhile, Elmina and the middle-aged examiner were speaking in hushed voices near the dungeon's entrance.

"And as you're no doubt aware, no one's ever even made it past the second floor of the Twilight Temple," Elmina continued. "You know why, don't you?"

"Because of the puzzle found there, right?"

"Yes, exactly."

Most dungeons were built around puzzles. There was no proceeding past a certain point without solving them.

The Twilight Temple was no different. The instant an adventurer descended the stairs to the second floor, a trap would be sprung and the adventurer would be stuck. The only way to escape the room was to solve the puzzle.

"Heh-heh... Solving the puzzle on the second floor is impossible. To succeed, you'd have to know what the puzzle was!"

Many an adventurer had tried their hand at the second floor's puzzle. But none of them had ever been able to crack it. And the reason was simple: The instructions to solve the puzzle were written in a language that no one alive knew how to read.

The theory was that the words were written in a long-forgotten language from an ancient civilization of magic...and all who had tried to decipher its meaning had failed.

How could one solve a puzzle without knowing *what* the puzzle was in the first place? Even worse, every time someone put forth an incorrect answer, monsters would appear. In other words, guessing at random wouldn't work, either.

"The only way back is to use a Wings of Return item to warp to the entrance. But the one I gave to Lorna Hermit was fake. Get it? She will surely be trapped on the second floor forever."

"Y-yes, but...was it truly necessary to go to such lengths to fail the girl?"

"Ex*cuse* me? Is a *peasant* like you with a garbage skill really complaining about the decision that I, Elmina Manaflame, retainer to the Guugelheit family, personally made?"

"I, um, seem to recall you besmirching the Guugelheit name very recently..."

"Wh-whatever! This will be the end of Lorna Hermit!"

If Elmina succeeded in sealing away a monster like that girl, she was certain to be commended by the Guugelheits. And that meant that Elmina would get to continue living the elite life after all.

"Ah-ha! Ha-ha-ha-ha! As if I would ever fear the likes of Lorna Hermit! After all, I was *born* to be an elite!"

Elmina cackled villainously. But as she laughed...

Rmmmmbbbbb! Rmmmmmbbb!

...the earth began to tremble violently. It was as though an enormous monster was on a rampage deep in the depths of the dungeon.

"................."

"Wh-what in the world?! Mistress Elmina, what do you suppose is—? M-Mistress Elmina?"

"...I hate this! I'm scared! I want to go home!"

"Mistress Elmina?!"

Meanwhile...

Lorna had already reached the fourth floor of the dungeon.

The entrance to the room had been sealed off with iron bars. But this proved no problem for Lorna.

"Uh, let's see. 'Touch the two crystals in the following order to open the door: Right, left, right, right, right, left.' And...there!"

Rmmmmmbbb!

A stone door parted, revealing a set of stairs leading down to the next level.

"Okay! It was just like the internet said! ♪"

And with that, Lorna had cleared the fourth floor.

Since each level only had a single puzzle to solve, making her way through the dungeon wasn't taking that much time at all. The fact that this dungeon was likely meant as a test of one's wisdom was of little concern to Lorna.

The puzzles aren't very challenging if you already know the answer.

Dealing with simple puzzles was much better than having to defeat a bunch of monsters.

I feel kinda bad, though... Sorry, everyone who made this dungeon!

Lorna apologized earnestly in the depths of her heart as she made her way to the next floor.

Chapter 7   I Tried Fighting the Dungeon Boss!

"Well... Here it is. The bottom floor."

Lorna had spent about twenty minutes in the dungeon when she reached the lowest level: the ninth floor.

Getting here was way, way too easy. It doesn't even feel real.

It had helped that the dungeon was primarily designed around solving puzzles and wasn't particularly large or deep. And since Lorna knew the answers to all the puzzles from the get-go, a leisurely walk through a handful of rooms was enough to take her to the bottom.

"But now I have to fight a boss, right? I hope I'll be okay..."

Lorna stood in front of a massive door. If she could defeat the boss on the other side and collect the Labyrinth Core, she would pass the adventurers exam.

"First things first—the internet!"

She opened the Wiki Guide page on the boss she was about to face. It contained a list of recommended skills and a detailed strategy for how to fight it. But Lorna hesitated.

Hmm, I dunno. This is just a bunch of information. It's kinda hard to get a sense for how strong this thing is going to be. I wish there was something more concrete. Like if someone could tell me what fighting it is like...

The moment that thought popped into her head, Lorna noticed something on the page.

"Huh...? Comments?"

She had never noticed it before, but at the bottom of the page was a collection of comments from different people.

Who would write something in a place like this...? thought Lorna, somewhat taken aback.

But if the internet was a bookshelf for the gods, that meant the ones who had written these comments were...

"These...must be conversations between the gods themselves."

Lorna swallowed hard. She was certain whatever was inscribed in this "comment section" would constitute a conversation of extra-dimensional proportions, the likes of which she couldn't begin to imagine.

Is...is it really okay for me to behold such hallowed words? Well, I've come this far... Okay! Here I go!

Lorna strengthened her resolve as her eyes moved down the screen to the comments section.

As for what was written there...

■ Discussion (84 comments)

#79: Anonymous Ninja
what do u mean u won lmaooo
get outta here with that crap bro. u must be braindead lol
freakin tryhard lolol get a life fr

#80: Anonymous Knight
okay w/e
you're just mad cause you know i'm right

#81: Anonymous NIGHT
Yo this guy's so mad right now I bet his face is red while he's typing lmfao

* * *

#82: Anonymous Ninja
pffft whatever bro, ive got no time for losers like u unlike you jobless basement dwellers i actually have shit to do lmao ive gotta get to work so c u later morons lol
btw if u keep tryin to pick fights with me im gonna doxx u so, keep fukn around n find out lol

#83: Anonymous Partier
What color are your panties???

#84: Anonymous Swordsman
Bruh, you need to log off.

"......................"

Lorna stared at the screen in shock, her mouth agape. When she finally spoke, her voice was trembling.

"Th-the gods... They're fighting...?"

She didn't understand the strange dialect they were using, but she was certain they were fighting a war beyond the ken of mere mortals like her.

I'm not sure what "lol" and "lmao" mean, but...they must be magical words used to cast some kind of spell!

There was much Lorna didn't understand. But for now...

"...Right, well. I'm just going to pretend I didn't see any of that."

Lorna scrolled down quickly and put the comments out of sight, then she passed her eyes over yet more words left by the gods.

"This boss is so damn weak man. I can't believe a weakass loser like this gives out S-Rank gear lmao"
"Man the opening movie for this one was peak."
"I no damage'd this guy at Level 1 and it was so easy."

"Have they seriously not fixed the safe spot on this boss yet?"
"Who cares. I just want them to fix the power creep on anything over S-Rank"
"You all seriously think they're ever going to fix the game balance in Etalia? Get real."

Lorna had trouble comprehending a lot of what she saw. But the fact that the boss was weak came through loud and clear.

Based on what the gods are saying...I guess this boss must be really weak.

One of them had even defeated it at Level 1.

Well... It's written on the internet. So it must be true. This makes me feel a lot better...

Lorna had yet to find any lies on the internet, so she felt confident it would be right this time as well. It also made perfect sense why this task had been chosen for the adventurers exam.

"Okay, then! Let's get this over with!"

She moved in front of the large door leading to the boss room.

"I'm pretty sure I need to say the key words in front of this door. Let's see... 'It is I, the one carved with the number of the beast,' right?"

As soon as she spoke those words, there was a tremendous rumbling, and the door opened on its own. The room on the other side was pitch-black.

"Huh? It's so dark. I can't see anything...," Lorna muttered, making her way into the center of the space. The moment she reached it...

Drip, drip, drip.

...water began to trickle down from above, falling right before her eyes.

Lorna looked up. That was when she saw it.

"Uh...?"

Right above her head was a massive gaping maw lined with countless teeth. What she had thought was a wall in front of her turned out to be the body of a gargantuan black dragon.

"......"

Lorna's mouth fell open, and her body froze stiff. Then, from behind her came a *slam*! She looked back and saw that the door had sealed her in.

"Uh... Uhhh... I'm s-s-stuck...?"

It seemed to be one of those "no leaving until the boss is defeated" type of situations.

Lorna turned timidly back around, and her eyes met those of the black dragon.

The black dragon's whole body was bound in golden chains, and it looked like a fearsome, wicked god of old. It reminded Lorna of a guard dog. Or rather, a guard dragon.

"Grrrraaaaarrrrrgghhh!!!"

The dragon's roar rocked the entire room and made it tremble and quake. The sound had hit Lorna at point-blank range.

"......"

Silently, she turned around to face the other direction.

"Nope, nope, nope. Nooo, thank yooooou! Wasn't this thing supposed to be weak?! How is this *weak*?! Open! Open uuuup!" she screamed, tears in her eyes, as she banged on the door.

But of course, the door refused to open. There was no running away from a boss fight.

D-did the internet lie to me?! But the internet's never lied to me! There's no way! Maybe...maybe this thing's only weak from the point of view of a god?!

As Lorna's mind raced, the black dragon lumbered toward her, ripping its chains from their moorings. The fight had already begun.

In a panic, Lorna turned her staff toward the dragon.

"Ahhhhh!!! Petit Ice! Petit Ice! Petit Ice!!!"

The ice formed a tremendous wave that assaulted the creature.

The fact that she had cast the same starter spell over and over in a panic did not change the fact that she was casting each one with an SSS-Rank staff.

The black dragon let out a pained roar and tried its best to maneuver out of the way of the icy barrage. Lorna took advantage of the opening.

"C-c'mon, internet!"

She manipulated the screen as she frantically ran around the room.

"I'm gonna die! I'm gonna die! I'm gonna diiiiie!!! I need to look up this dragon or else I'll— Wh-wha—?! I think I pressed the wrong thing! Oh no, oh no! How do I go baaaaack?!"

♥♥Registration complete!♥♥
♡ Adult content agreement confirmed!
♡ Terms of use confirmed!
♡ Age confirmed!
[!] Payment must be received within three days of registration.
Contact us: XXX-XXX-XXXX
*If you registered by mistake, CLICK HERE.

"Gyaaaaah?!"

Lorna's face turned crimson as she frantically tapped the CLICK HERE button.

[!] VIRUS DETECTED! [!]
Warning: Your system is about to crash!
To delete, press OK now!

* * *

"Whyyyyyyyyy?!"

"Grrrrrrooooaaaaarrrr!"

"Aaaaaahhhh!!! Petit Ice! Petit Ice! Petit Iiiiiiice!!!"

This went on for a while.

Despite her panic, however, Lorna eventually managed to find the information she was after.

■ **Boss: Apocalypse Dragon Ragnadrek**
Spawn Location: The Twilight Temple
Level: 83
Weaknesses: Fire, Ice, Light. Weak points in the stomach and wings.
Resistances: Dark, Poison, Debuffs
Rewards: Apocalypse Dragon equipment (guaranteed), Item Box Expansion +50, Apocalypse Dragon Gem (100 percent), Apocalypse Dragon Scale (70 percent), Apocalypse Dragon Wing Membrane (20 percent), Apocalypse Dragon Crown (7 percent)

◇ Details: A Hard difficulty boss that can be fought after clearing part one of the story.

This boss has been present since the first version and is the weakest of the Hard bosses. Flashes are very effective at blinding it. It also has several weak points to exploit. Finally, the boss area contains a safe spot for avoiding damage.

"Pant... Pant... Safe spot?"

Lorna, still flustered, swiped her hand repeatedly at the screen in an attempt to find more info on this "safe spot."

"The safe spot is...behind the stone altar? Um... Oh! Over there!"

At the back of the room was a space that looked like it might be used for rituals. According to the internet, the area behind the altar at the top of the stone stairs was a safe spot.

Lorna had no time to think things through.

"Reckless Rush!"

She activated her Reckless Boots' equip skill and flew across the room and up the stone stairs. She couldn't brake in time, so she stopped herself another way—by slamming against the wall.

"*Huff... Huff...* This is the safe spot?"

There was nothing in the space aside from the stone altar. And it wasn't particularly high up, either. She couldn't imagine it providing much defense against the dragon's attacks.

Looking back, she saw that the black dragon was right on her tail.

"Grrrrrrooooaaaaarrrr!"

Its roar was filled with rage. And from within the dragon's gaping maw, Lorna could see flames beginning to build. She had read about this on the internet. It was the action the boss took before it unleashed its breath attack.

"Waaaahhh!"

Lorna panicked and slid behind the stone altar. At almost the same exact instant, the dragon launched its attack.

GROOOOOOOOOOOOOOOOAAAARRR!!!

The dragon's roar was followed by a beam of light, its golden hue reminiscent of the twilight sky.

"Huh...?"

Lorna was confused. For some strange reason, the dragon's breath attack didn't reach all the way to the stone altar. It might have had something to do with the angle from which it was launched. Or maybe it had collided with some kind of barrier. She couldn't be sure.

What's more, the black dragon didn't show any signs of trying to climb up after her. Apparently, the stairs were too small for it.

Chapter 7: I Tried Fighting the Dungeon Boss!

In other words, the dragon couldn't get close enough to use any physical attacks, nor could it reach Lorna with its breath attack.

"Th-this spot... It really *is* safe."

Lorna heaved a sigh of relief.

The black dragon continued to ceaselessly fire off its breath attack. But there was nothing to fear.

Lorna assumed that whoever had been keeping this dragon here (maybe as a pet?) had carefully calculated the layout of the area so as to create this safe spot.

If I stand here and hit it with long-range attacks, then...

She could win.

Filled with determination, Lorna pointed her staff at the black dragon.

"Okay, first up—Terra Drain!"

Lorna sapped the boss's MP, draining it of its ability to fight.

"Next up! Petit Ice!"

The internet had said the black dragon was weak to ice, so Lorna poured all the MP she'd just drained into a barrage of ice spells. At this point, the black dragon was little more than a massive target.

"Next uuup... A little break."

Lorna sat down behind the altar and took out the packed lunch she had brought with her. She'd been walking a lot today, and this seemed like as good a time as any to recharge.

Mmm. The sweetness of this Ipple pie is just what I needed.

All the while, the black dragon continued to roar and rampage nearby. And after Lorna had finished her Ipple pie and Ipple juice...

"Okay! Time for round two!"

...she went right back to pelting the boss with ice spells.

Then, after Lorna had cast the same ice spell many times, something changed.

"Wh-whoa! It's flying!"

The black dragon tore apart its chains and took to the air.

"Oh, I remember reading about this. When its HP gets low, its attack pattern changes…"

She wondered why it didn't simply go all out from the get-go. Perhaps it had been created in such a way that it was only able to unleash its full power in an emergency. Luckily, the internet had Lorna covered when it came to dealing with this new pattern.

◇ **Strategy: When its HP drops below 50 percent, the dragon will begin to attack from the air and strike with its chains.**

Dealing with the dragon while it is airborne is tricky, so knock it out of the sky with a flash of light.

The range of its breath attack is also increased during this phase, and it inflicts Poison, Paralysis, and Confusion. Get ready to dodge as soon as it starts charging its breath attack, or retreat to the safe spot.

"Um, right! When it starts to fly, I use…Petit Flash!"

Bang!

A flash of light erupted above her. The black dragon groaned and fell out of the air. As it writhed around on the ground, Lorna launched another Terra Drain followed by another barrage of Petit Ice.

Any time it seemed like the dragon was about to use its breath attack, she would carefully hide behind the altar. And whenever it took to the air, she would use Petit Flash.

"All right, looks like I've got its movements down!"

Lorna did a small fist pump.

According to the internet, the gods called this "having the high ground."

Seriously, though… Is this dragon just really dumb? Why does it keep repeating the same things over and over again…?

It was almost as if its movements followed a set pattern.

I kind of feel bad for it. It's like I'm bullying the poor thing.
Of course, it would kill Lorna if she didn't kill it first. So she took a deep breath and…

"Petit Ice!"

…unleashed a full-strength blast of ice magic.
Crack-crickle-crackk!!!
Ice enveloped the room and froze the black dragon completely. It seemed her final attack had done the trick. The boss exploded in a huge burst of mana light and disappeared, leaving behind a block of ice in the shape of its body.

Defeated Apocalypse Dragon Ragnadrek! You gained 66,600 EXP!
LEVEL UP! Lv. 22 → Lv. 42
SKILL UP! Giant Killer II → Giant Killer III
SKILL UP! Magic V → Magic VII
You learned the Petit Darkness and Petit Barrier starter spells!
You learned the Dragon Slayer I skill!
Item Box slots have been expanded by 50!
Obtained Title: "Apocalyptic Conqueror"

Text recording the experience points and a host of other rewards Lorna had just obtained flashed by her eyes one after another.
And that meant…
"I…did it? I beat the dungeon?"
The moment Lorna spoke those words aloud…
Poof!
…a treasure chest appeared on top of the stone altar.

"Whoa! Wh-what's that?" she said, reeling.

Um, I guess this is my reward? But who would leave something like this here? And...why? Actually...where did this thing even come from? How did it appear?

Indeed, the treasure chest had manifested out of thin air.

Though, come to think of it, the internet did mention there would be a reward for defeating the boss.

Upon recalling this, Lorna checked the internet again.

Let's see... "After defeating Apocalypse Dragon Ragnadrek, it will drop a piece of Apocalypse Dragon equipment that corresponds to the battle style you used during combat." Hmm... I don't really understand what this "Item Box Expansion +50" part means, though...

That hardly mattered, however. At the end of the day, Lorna would take whatever rewards she could get. Besides, who could resist the allure of opening a treasure chest?

She reached out, eyes brimming with excitement, and threw open the lid.

"Wooow! A robe!"

She pulled out a jet-black robe. Talk about luck—this was exactly what she had been hoping for.

"Yesss! I got the equipment I wanted most!"

Lorna's DEF was so low that it had become a source of constant anxiety. Even a small scratch from the black dragon could have easily killed her. But now all of that was in the past.

Yep, yep! A high attack stat is all well and good, but there's nothing like having good defense.

Lorna wasted no time equipping her new robe and checking out her stats.

■ Lorna Hermit, Lv. 42
HP: 164/164
MP: 96,660/276

ATK: 44 (+360)
DEF: 90 (+746)
M-ATK: 173 (+3,600)
MIND: 173 (+1,666)
SPD: 88 (+300)
LUCK: 90

◆ Equipment
Weapon: Staff of World Tree (SSS)
Armor: Apocalypse Dragon Ragnarobe (S)
Armor: Reckless Boots (B)

◆ Skills
Internet (SSS)
Terra Drain (SSS)
Enchanted Wings (S)
Reckless Rush (B)
Magic VII (D)
Giant Killer III (D)
Art of Slaughter I (E)
Dragon Slayer I (C)

◆ Titles
The Abandoned One
Yggdrasil's Chosen
Calamity Witch
Lord Slayer
Apocalyptic Conqueror

"W-wow... I've gotten pretty strong..."

Lorna hadn't taken a good look at the level-up screen when it displayed a moment ago. She was only just now noticing that she had shot up twenty whole levels.

At Level 40, I'm in the same league as some of the strongest warriors in the kingdom...

That made her plenty powerful without even factoring in the modifiers from her equipment. And now her DEF was off the charts, and her MIND had somehow already hit four digits.

"I wasn't even trying that hard..."

It felt like Lorna was rapidly moving away from the bounds of humanity into something beyond. But setting that aside for the time being...

"This robe was called the Apocalypse Dragon Ragnarobe, right? Let's see..."

She decided to focus on looking up her new equipment instead.

■ **Equipment (Robe): Apocalypse Dragon Ragnarobe**
Rank: S
Type: Robe
Price: 66,600,000,000 shil
Effect: DEF +666, MIND +1,666
Poison, Blindness, Instant Death Resistance +66 percent
Dark Resistance +66 percent
◇ **Equip Skill: Enchanted Wings (S)**
Effect: Grants the target Winged status (lasts until canceled). Winged status allows target to fly (ignoring all terrain effects).
◇ **Details: Apocalypse Dragon Ragnadrek used this robe when he was a human king.**

This flight-bestowing garb is a symbol of the king's avarice and his desire to make the very heavens his own. In the end, it was sealed underground along with its owner.

Using the robe's equip skill, Enchanted Wings, enables the player to fly directly to the starting location of a variety of Hard

difficulty content. During combat, it allows you to attack from above, letting you strike from safety at any time and effectively breaking the game's balance.

It is important to note, however, that controls when Winged are difficult to master. It's likely to give you a horrible case of motion sickness and make you want to throw up. Caution is advised.

Okay, well... It's strong; I know that much.

Lorna was completely lost, as usual. But the main point seemed to be that the robe came with an equip skill called Enchanted Wings. And who could ignore the allure of trying out a new skill?

"All right, here goes! Enchanted Wings!" she called out cheerfully.

Two wings of white light spread out from Lorna's back.

"Wow! I'm like an ange—eeehhlllll?!"

The moment the words left her lips, her body began to float upward.

"Uhhh?!"

She floated all the way to the ceiling, bumped her head, and fell back down to the floor. Thankfully, her DEF was so high that she barely felt a thing.

"Th-this is going to take a lot of practice to get used to..."

Being able to fly *sounded* useful, but this skill was clearly going to be a tough one to master.

"Anyway. I wonder what this other thing I got is. It says Item Box Expansion +50, but what could that possibly mean?"

Item Box Expansion +50. That was what the reward screen had said, in any case. But rummaging through the treasure chest, Lorna couldn't find anything inside that seemed to fit that description.

"Hmm. Maybe I need to call it out like an incantation? Let's see... Item Box!"

She'd tried saying the words out of pure curiosity, but the moment she did, her staff disappeared from her hand and a screen appeared in front of her eyes.

Inventory: 1/50

"Uh... I guess this is where my staff went."

In a frame underneath the screen, she could see an icon that looked like a staff. She tapped it out of curiosity and—*poof*—her staff appeared in her hand.

"Wh-whoa! It's back! What's going on? This is *so* convenient!"

She was able to figure out how it worked in no time at all. Essentially, it was a skill that let her keep her things in a pocket dimension.

"This is...totally amazing!"

It had been bundled with her other rewards like a forgettable extra, but this would make carrying her things around infinitely easier. And now she no longer had to worry about her high-ranking gear getting stolen.

With something like this, Lorna could plunder and smuggle to her heart's content. Not that she would, of course.

"In that case..."

Lorna eyed the massive gem enshrined in the stone altar. She guessed it was the thing powering the whole dungeon—the Labyrinth Core. With her new skill, it would be a cinch to bring it back and complete her task for the exam.

"Okay, then! Item Box!" she called, reaching out to touch the Labyrinth Core. As soon as her fingers brushed it—*poof*—it was gone.

She looked at her Item Box again and confirmed it had been added: Twilight Temple Labyrinth Core xi. She would have no problem bringing it back to the entrance now.

"All right! Time to head back!"

She was still in the middle of the exam. If she didn't return quickly, the proctor would fail her for taking too much time. That said, she would also fail if she used an item to return to the entrance.

Looks like it's time to put Enchanted Wings to use.

She thought back to the path she had taken to the boss room. The dungeon was ripe with potential shortcuts now that she could fly. It was almost as if the place had been designed for her to try out her new skill.

"Okay, one more time! Enchanted Wings!"

Once again, wings of light grew out of Lorna's back, and she headed off toward the dungeon's entrance.

Meanwhile...

Just what is going on in here...? wondered Elmina Manaflame, the exam's proctor, as she took a step into the Twilight Temple.

Ever since Lorna Hermit had descended into the dungeon, the very earth had begun to quake and tremble ceaselessly. Elmina had also sensed a tremendous amount of mana and cold air flowing out from deep inside the dungeon.

Something wasn't right.

The other examinees had already been evacuated. But Elmina, as guild master, had little choice but to investigate the cause of the disturbances. And she was not at all prepared for what she saw inside.

"...Huh?! What...what happened here...?"

The dungeon was frozen solid. Entire hallways were encased in ice. Here and there she saw rows upon rows of monsters turned into frozen sculptures, their faces twisted in horror.

There was only one person who could be behind something like this, and yet...

Im...impossible!

Elmina had never heard of magic so powerful. Judging by the residual mana around her, the magic used to do this must have cost thousands of MP. No human was capable of such a feat. And what's more...

"...Ah! B-but how...?!"

Elmina came upon the door leading down to the third floor. It had been thrown open. Many adventurers had taken on this dungeon, but no one had *ever* gotten past the second floor. Elmina's entire plan hinged on trapping Lorna Hermit there. And yet...

"She...she made it through..."

It was inconceivable. There was no way to solve the second-floor puzzle unless you could decipher the mysterious instructions.

And yet the puzzle had been solved. And in such a short amount of time.

D-don't tell me... She can't possibly have cleared the dungeon...right?

Most adventurers treated dungeons merely as places to gather materials—and they tended to stick to the first few levels to do so, staying in areas where there were no traps or puzzles.

To even attempt to clear one, a person would need an exorbitant amount of items, traversal skills, and *a whole lot of time*. A dungeon was not something one cleared like this, all alone, and with absolutely no preparation.

"...Ah!"

Suddenly, Elmina felt a chill run down her spine. It felt like someone had grasped her heart with a frozen hand. She instinctually understood what it meant.

Something, or *someone*, was there.

Elmina looked to the left and right...but she couldn't see anyone. Yet the feeling was unmistakable—there was an overwhelming presence nearby.

"M-Mana Scan! ...?!"

The moment she activated the skill, she noticed it.

An enormous amount of mana filled the area. It seemed to be coming from every direction. Whoever it was, Elmina was already surrounded by their mana. And yet...she couldn't see them anywhere.

"Ah... Ngh..."

She couldn't breathe. Her teeth began to chatter uncontrollably, and she was filled with a primal sense of fear.

Just then, something passed before her eyes. A white feather had fallen from above.

...A feather?

That was when Elmina realized something: There was one place she had yet to look. This mana had to be coming from *there*.

So Elmina slowly tilted her head up, and...

"................Ah..."

...a profound sense of despair overtook her.

A shadow was looking down at her. It was floating in the air on divine wings of light.

It's...her...

Elmina knew all too well the identity of this creature beyond mortal comprehension.

It was Lorna Hermit.

What? ...Has she gotten even stronger? Is this Lorna Hermit's second form? Or maybe...this was her true form all along?

Lorna was now draped in a sinister robe of the darkest black and had wings of light growing from her back. What's more, the mana her body exuded had increased by an unfathomable amount. It was as though she had feasted on the dungeon's mana and made it her own.

I... I have to get out of here, thought Elmina. But her legs wouldn't move.

She felt like a tiny ant being glared at by a dragon.

As Elmina stood in place, frozen in panic...

"Oh! Miss Examiner! ♪"

"...?!"

Fwoosh!

...Lorna tore through the air at a tremendous speed and, in an instant, descended in front of her.

Oh...

This display brought Elmina to an unfortunate realization: There was no running away from Lorna Hermit.

"Look! I brought you the Labyrinth Core, just like you asked! ♪"

Lorna held her hand, and...

"...?!"

Fwoomp.

...the space around her hand warped and twisted. Suddenly, a massive gem appeared in Lorna's palm.

Wh-what was that?! Did she just use spatial magic? That's the stuff of legends! Th-there are no known skills with that kind of power! And that includes A-Ranks!

And more importantly, the gem in Lorna's hand—there was no mistaking it. It was the fabled Labyrinth Core. There was no chance it was a fake, either. The enormous amount of mana seeping out of it was proof of that.

Sh-she actually got the Labyrinth Core...?! Then it's true?! She already cleared the entire dungeon?!

Elmina's mind went blank. She was so disoriented and confused that she thought she might throw up. But she knew one thing—everything she had ever thought she knew about the world had been completely upended.

Lorna held out the legendary Labyrinth Core for Elmina as though it were some common bauble.

"So…I guess I pass the exam, huh?" said Lorna with a big grin.

Elmina felt so much pressure emanating from that grin that she broke out in a cold sweat.
I… I have to fail you… If I don't, then my elite life plan…will be…
She had to fail Lorna at all costs. Her entire lifestyle depended on it.
Tears streamed down Elmina's face. All she could muster was a nod.

"You…you…pass…," she replied, deflated.

It had all been for naught. There was no way for her to fail Lorna.
Why is a monster like this even taking the adventurers exam…? And why did those damned Guugelheits disown her in the first place…?
Elmina didn't understand. Nothing made sense to her. But she knew her actions today would mean the end of her relationship with the Guugelheit family. Her elite lifestyle was over.
She didn't regret her decision, though. The reason was simple— Lorna was far more terrifying than the Guugelheits could ever be.

"Oh, right!" said Lorna suddenly. She placed her hand on Elmina's shoulder.

"Your life… You should take care of it, okay?"

"…Um, what?"
"If you're not careful, Miss Elmina… Well, you might die. And sooner than you expect."
"……"
Elmina nodded furiously in response.

Lorna, seeming satisfied, flashed Elmina a smile before walking away.

A few moments later, when the final echoes of Lorna's footsteps died down, Elmina collapsed in a heap.

She...she's going to murder me...

The girl's words had been a clear warning. Lorna Hermit did not take kindly to Elmina's attempt to trap her.

"Try that again and I'll kill you. Got it?"

Lorna's smile had said it all. There was no other way to interpret it.

I think, pondered Elmina, face blank, *I need to go home. I miss my hometown.*

Meanwhile...

Miss Elmina sure is kind. She must have worried about me and entered the dungeon to make sure I was okay. What a nice thing to do.

Lorna hummed as she made her way back to the dungeon's entrance. An internet window floated just ahead of her.

■ **Character: Elmina Manaflame**

Guild master of the Aiphoné Adventurers Guild.

Wielder of the A-Rank skill, Inferno Magic. Also known as the Witch of Conflagration.

Elmina is an elite spellcaster and retainer of the Guugelheit family.

She is very popular in the fandom, especially in a certain section of the fan art community.

MASSIVE SPOILERS BELOW!

Elmina dies in Part 1, Chapter 5.

* * *

I still can't believe the internet knows when people are going to die... Elmina's such a kind person; I'd really hate for anything to happen to her.

Lorna didn't understand the bit about *when* Elmina was supposed to die, but now that she'd warned her of her fate, Lorna hoped the guild master would find some way to avoid it.

Chapter 8 I Became an Adventurer!

The morning after Lorna passed the adventurers exam, she returned to the guild headquarters to pick up her documentation.

"M-Miss Lorna Hermit... H-h-here is your adventurers card... Eh-heh..."

"Yaaay!"

Lorna took the shiny new card from Elmina, and the latter continued her explanation.

"Th-the adventurer ranks are as follows, from lowest to highest: Iron, Bronze, Silver, Gold, Mythril, and Orichalcum... S-so you'll be starting out as Iron ra—"

Snap!

Lorna crushed the brand-new card in the palm of her hand.

"......"

It broke into countless pieces. One of them grazed Elmina's face, which was still frozen in a cordial smile.

"Wh-whoa!" Lorna exclaimed. "I'm so, so sorry! I leveled up so fast in such a short time that I guess I don't know my own strength..."

"Please... Please don't kill me..."

"Huh? What do you mean?"

For some reason, tears were running down Elmina's cheeks. Lorna peered at her in confusion. Maybe the guild master was just tired.

"Would it be possible for you to...make me a new one?" she asked.

"Oh, but of course...! We'll make you a new one right away... Ngh..."

"Why are you crying?"

"Oh, this? Ngh. It's just allergies..."

With that, Elmina meekly retreated to the back room of the reception area.

I always assumed that people with high-ranking skills would be mean and stuck-up... But Elmina is just such a kind person.

Not only had she defended Lorna when everyone in the testing hall was bad-mouthing her, but she had even gone down into the dungeon to check up on her.

And now Lorna had rudely destroyed the adventurers card Elmina had only just given her. Despite that, Elmina hadn't gotten angry at all. To Lorna, she seemed like a kind and capable elder sister.

"S-sorry to keep you waiting...," Elmina said, reemerging a short while later. "H-here's your new card..."

The card Elmina held in her hand was made of bronze.

"Hmm? But isn't this a Bronze rank card? I thought you said everyone started out at Iron rank."

"W-well, you see, Miss Lorna, your exam was slightly more difficult than usual. So I thought it only right to give you a corresponding boost in rank."

"...?"

Lorna was a bit confused. But as long as it wasn't a mistake, then she supposed there wasn't a problem.

Satisfied, she reached out to receive her adventurers card. But as she did...

"Ah-*achoo!*"

Snap!
Once again, before Elmina's very eyes, Lorna shattered her new card to pieces.

"Please...please, forgive me..."

And so Lorna had to ask Elmina—who was sobbing uncontrollably for some reason—to make her a new card yet again. And despite the fact that issuing a new card usually incurred a fee, Elmina said she would waive it especially for Lorna.

Wow. Miss Elmina sure is kind. I hope I can show her my gratitude someday.

Lorna's show of gratitude would almost certainly lead to more suffering for Elmina Manaflame. But that's a story for another time.

In the end, Lorna received a third new card that day. And for some reason, it was Silver rank.

"Wh-what's the deal? Why's Elmina Manaflame acting like a pushover...?"

"That girl was issued a Silver rank card on her first day? What kind of connections does she have?!"

"She must be related to someone in the royal court or something..."

"Damn. She looks innocent enough, but it's probably best not to mess with her..."

She might have drawn a lot of attention, but Lorna was finally an official adventurer.

"And that's how I got my adventurers card."

Shortly after the events at the Adventurers Guild, Lorna went to see Reinharte to show off her shiny new license.

"Whoa! I'd expect nothing less from you, Lorna!"

His eyes sparkled with pride, as if Lorna's achievement were his own. But then he went on to say, "I'm so impressed you were able to pass an exam proctored by Elmina Manaflame. You're amazing, Lorna!"

"......"

"And you've jumped right to Silver rank! That's unheard of! You're amazing, Lorna!"

"......"

"Yet despite all that, you're still so calm and cool. I swear, you're simply amazing, Lorna!"

"......"

"Is something the matter, Lorna? If anything is troubling you, don't hesitate to tell me. I, Reinharte Highwind, would gladly walk through fire, water, gales, or snow for you. I am ready to put my life on the line to help!"

"Um, well…"

"Yes?"

"I don't remember you being so…*positive* last time."

Reinharte had been much more subdued the last time they met. He no longer wore a helmet low over his eyes, and a cheerful smile graced his face.

"Why, it's all thanks to you, Lorna! You healed my leg, and now I have a new lease on life!"

"Oh… So it's because of me that you're acting like this…?"

Reinharte had been incessantly rambling like a child meeting his hero for the first time.

"Until I met you, Lorna, I was little more than a living corpse. But then you came along and saved me! You've brought hope back into my life. Or rather, you've reminded me just how beautiful this

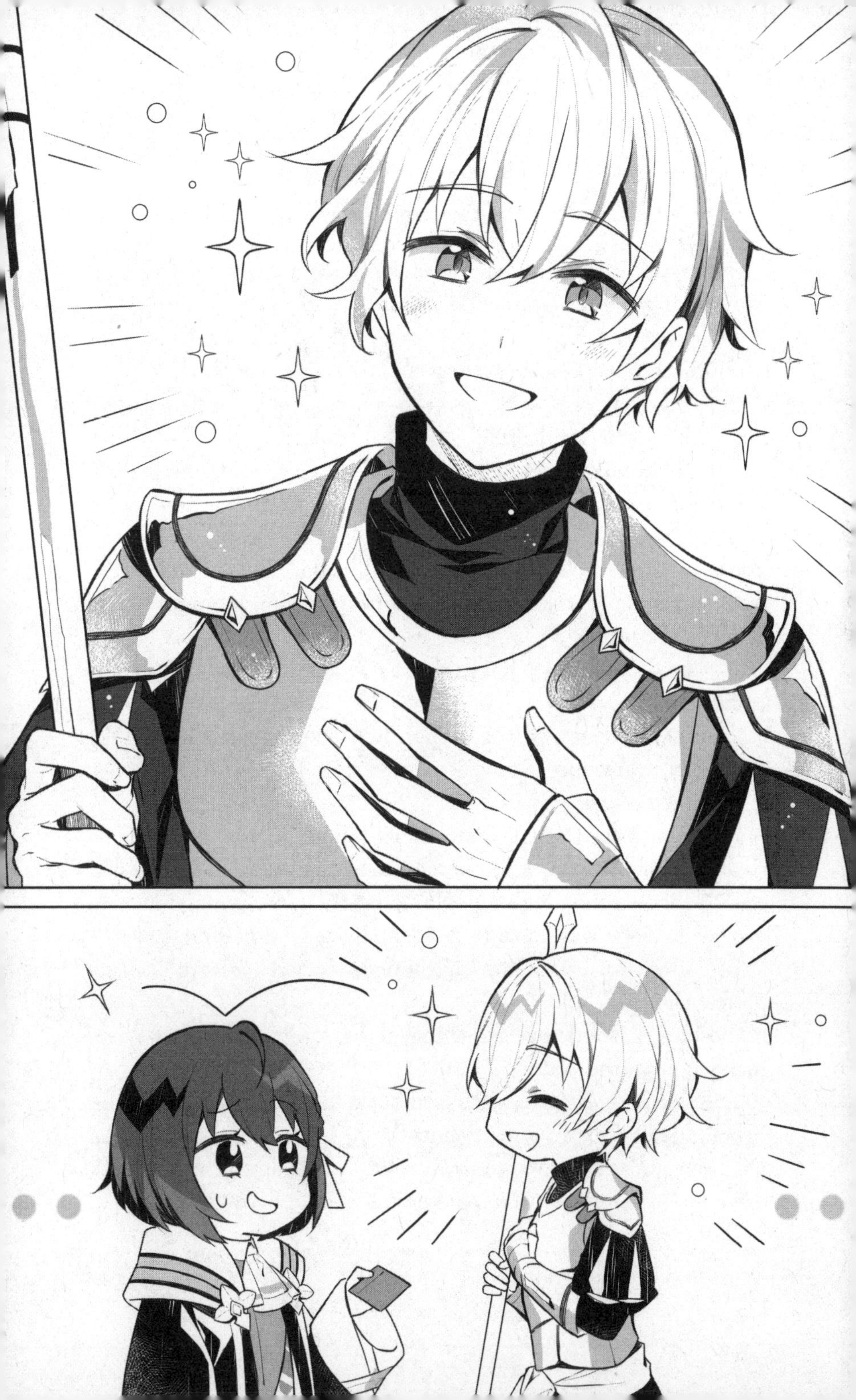

world can be. Oh, I would love nothing more than to become the kind of adventurer who rescues people. Just like you, Lorna!"

"Um. Right..."

Lorna had never intended to *save* the young man, so his excessive show of gratitude caught her off guard.

This guy's kinda creepy...

His display was kind of putting her off.

"And you're already working on your first quest as an adventurer, huh? You're amazing, Lorna!"

"Uh. Right. Well, it's just collecting some medicinal herbs. It's really no big deal."

"Well, now! Collecting medicinal herbs. That's amazing, Lorna. You're incredibly powerful, but you're still so humble. To think you'd take on such a practical request just to help someone out. You're amazing, Lorna!"

"No, no. I just thought it would be a good idea to start with something simple, is all..."

"Still doing things in the proper order, despite your incredible skills. You're amazing, Lorna!"

This guy is so annoying...

This would be Lorna's first official job as an adventurer. The thought of failing her first quest stressed her out, and she wasn't exactly thrilled about fighting. Not to mention, one wrong move in a battle and she was liable to accidentally cause a natural disaster. When all was said and done, collecting some herbs seemed like the perfect choice.

"Besides, I heard that collecting herbs is a really good way to make money," she said.

"...Really? *Collecting herbs?*" Reinharte looked at her, confused. "Though, now that you mention it, I've heard that a strange illness has been spreading through town recently... I suppose that would drive up demand for medicinal herbs. I should have known you'd pick the request most likely to benefit the town. You're incredible, Lorna!"

Reinharte seemed satisfied with his conclusion that Lorna was doing this out of the goodness of her heart. In truth, Lorna's goal was one hundred percent financial. She needed money. But she wasn't about to correct him.

"But aren't you worried about going on an adventure all alone?" he asked. "It could be dangerous. There are so many things to do—scouting for enemies, combat, carrying all your items. Having to do it solo seems like quite the balancing act."

"You think so?"

Lorna didn't know much about the finer details of adventuring. Until just a few days ago, things like adventure and combat were completely irrelevant to her life. And so far, everything she'd learned had come from the internet. As a result, what seemed like common sense to Lorna was, in fact, quite absurd. But she had no way of knowing that.

"Well, I'll probably be fine," she said. "I've got a skill that lets me fly around in the sky, so if things get bad, I can just fly away."

"It lets you...fly?"

"Yup."

Lorna demonstrated by using her recently acquired skill—Enchanted Wings.

Wings of light spread out from Lorna's back. She looked like some kind of angel.

"……"

Reinharte froze in place.

"All right, I should probably get going," she said.

"……"

"Um, Mr. Reinharte?"

"Uh... Huh? Oh! R-right... Of course. Well, then. Safe travels."

"Okay."

And with that, Lorna took to the skies and flew away. Reinharte watched in shock as she soared through the heavens.

"Has Lorna…been an angel this whole time…?"

When Elmina first saw Lorna's wings, she hadn't reacted at all (because she was petrified by despair). As a result, Lorna had erroneously assumed that flight skills were fairly common. But the truth was: The idea sounded completely unbelievable to most people.

Reinharte had traveled all across the land on his adventurers, and he had *never* heard of such a skill.

"Y-you know, whenever I talk to Lorna, I can't help but feel that the world is much larger than I ever imagined…"

Reinharte put on a wry smile as he thought about Lorna. Her very existence seemed to defy logic.

"All right… First, I'm going to focus on my rehab. Then I'll work hard to get as close to her level as I can."

Having said his piece, Reinharte went back to swinging his spear.

Chapter 9   I Gathered an Infinite Number of Herbs!

Shortly after she parted ways with Reinharte, Lorna was flying through the sky on wings of light, headed for Ipple Woods.

"What's that up in the sky? A new type of monster?"

"Whatever it is, it's fast!"

"Isn't that the new girl, Lorna Hermit? Everyone's talking about her."

"I never knew there was a skill that let you fly through the air..."

Lorna was soaring over a grassy plain, giving the adventurers below a perfect view of her. They all watched in amazement, but Lorna was too high above them to notice.

Eventually, she alighted in the woods.

"Phew." Lorna sighed, deactivating her wings of light. And within seconds...

"G-guh...gonna be sick..."

She reached up and held a hand over her mouth. Her face was ghostly pale as an intense nausea overtook her. It felt like when she got sick from riding in a carriage. She still wasn't used to flying, clearly.

Traveling through the sky is handy and all, but...I should really try to figure out how to keep steady while I'm up there...

But after a short rest, she was ready to go again.

"Okay! Time to gather some medicinal herbs!"

Lorna was ready to get down to business and start harvesting.

Despite being a lot of work, gathering herbs wasn't seen as a very rewarding endeavor. For that reason, few adventurers were willing to bother with such quests.

"*Wha—? Gathering medicinal herbs...? I can't say there's much money to be made there... Wh-what exactly are you planning...?*"

Elmina had seemed doubtful when Lorna volunteered to take the quest.

But as long as I've got the internet, I'll be able to find all the best gathering spots...

Of course, Lorna was only looking for one specific type of herb. She popped open the internet and let it guide her to the nearest spot. And after a bit of searching...

"Here's one!"

...she found a single medicinal herb growing out of the ground.

This was the same place where she had stumbled upon some Phantom Leafs before fighting the Lord of the Woods.

■ **Item: Phantom Leaf**
Type: Material
Price: 50,000 shil
Effect: None
◇ **Details: A rare medicinal herb from the Magic Forest that grows in very small quantities.**

Can be used as a material in high-grade healing items such as Elixirs and Elven Nostrum. Also used as an event item in the side quest, *The Toxic Ambitions of Dr. Zariché.*

Heh... Heh-heh-heh... If I collect a bunch of these, I'll make a ton of money!

Lorna was grinning like a fool.

She had found out how to make a bundle on them only the night before. After clearing the dungeon, she'd retired to an inn and was playing around on the internet.

That dragon was pretty dangerous… I should really do more research before I jump into danger so I can keep a calm head in the moment…

And so Lorna began to do a bit more research into the world around her.

Huh… According to this, "Adventurers exploring ruins the world over have accidentally caused the king of an ancient magical civilization to be resurrected along with his army of demons. Even now, their schemes for world domination are underway." That sounds really bad… I feel like someone should probably do something about it. But wow, there's just so much I don't know about the world. I wish I could ask someone about some of this stuff… Wait, hold on.

That was when Lorna first noticed it.

Is this what I think it is…? It looks like I can post comments here, too.

Internet comment sections were the gathering places of the gods. And that meant that if Lorna posted her own question…she could tap directly into their divine power. Essentially, she could *cheat*.

I-if the church ever found out that I have a direct line to the gods…things could get weird. They might try to worship me as a saint or something. Looks like I've discovered another facet of the internet's fearsome power…

But right now, Lorna needed to draw upon that power. There was simply too much about the world she didn't know.

I-is it really all right for me to just ask the gods a question, though…?

She wasn't sure if they would even bother responding to the pitiful concerns of a tiny human like her.

She anxiously rolled the idea around in her mind until, twenty minutes later, she'd more or less put her thoughts in order.

"I...wonder if what I've written is okay. Ngh... Actually, wait. Forget it. I shouldn't. But then again, I've already written everything out, so... A-all right, here I gooo!"

Lorna steeled her resolve and pressed the POST button.

With a *click*, the screen transitioned to the comment section. Her question had been added at the bottom.

■ Discussion (67 comments)
#67: im lorna
im in aiphone now and i need money. is there a good way to makes ome?

"I... I did it. I asked the gods a question," she said with an anxious gulp.

There was no turning back now.

I hope I wasn't accidentally rude or anything. What am I going to do if I've offended them...? And I asked them how to make money, of all things...! Oh boy, I'm so nervous...

All sorts of anxieties filled Lorna's mind. Her heart was pounding. She stared at the screen for a few minutes, and...

"Oh! I got some responses already!"

She refreshed the screen and found that a number of new comments had appeared. She was sure the responses would be full of divine wisdom to guide her path forward.

Nervously, she scrolled down to read them. And this is what she saw:

■ Discussion (68 comments)
#68: Anonymous Partier
First, take your clothes off.

"Wh-whaaaat?!"

Chapter 9: I Gathered an Infinite Number of Herbs!

* * *

■ Discussion (69 comments)
#69: Anonymous NIGHT
moar! MOAR!!

"What does that even mean?!"

■ Discussion (70 comments)
#70: Anonymous Otaku
To be fair, you have to have a very high IQ to understand Etalia. The battles are extremely subtle, and without a solid grasp of theoretical physics most of the mechanics will go over a typical player's head. There's also Lucia's outlook, which is deftly woven into her characterization- her personal philosophy draws heavily from Dan Simmons's literature, for instance. The fans understand this stuff; they have the intellectual capacity to truly appreciate the depths of the game, to realize that it's not just fun- it says something deep about LIFE. As a consequence people who dislike Etalia truly ARE idiots- of course they wouldn't appreciate, for instance, the humor in Elmina's existential catchphrase "live the elite lifestyle," which itself is a reference to post-Eva metafiction. I'm smirking right now just imagining one of those addlepated simpletons scratching their heads in confusion as the developers' genius wit unfolds itself on their screens. What fools... How I pity them lolololol

".....................Huh."
Lorna turned away from the screen.
"Whatever the gods are thinking, it's clearly way over my head. Their speech sounds like something out of a higher dimension... That last one even had what looked like a curse at the end..."
Lorna was starting to worry she wouldn't get any information she could actually use. Until...

* * *

■ **Discussion (71 comments)**
#71: Anonymous Swordsman
Y'all seriously need to log off smh.
You sound like you're new, im lorna.
If you need to make some cash, you should go to the Ipple Woods and duplicate some Phantom Leafs.

"Duplicate?"

And that was how a kindly god taught Lorna a way to gather an unlimited number of medicinal herbs.

She had a hard time believing it was possible to duplicate an herb an unlimited number of times, of course. But then again, the internet had never lied before. So she figured this, too, must be the truth.

"Okay!"

With that, Lorna turned to face the Phantom Leaf.

"First, I give the leaf some water with a watering can. This makes it 'gatherable.' Then I pick only the leaves, making sure not to cut the root. As long as I leave the root alone, the herb will have one HP left. And then"—Lorna pointed her staff at the plant—"Petit Heal!"

Boi-oing! Another herb sprouted from the ground.

"Wh-whoa... It really worked. I can grow as many as I want like this."

Using this process on a common herb wouldn't be worth the MP consumption required. In fact, it might end up costing more money than it made. But when applied to a high-value item like the Phantom Leaf, the return on her investment would be high enough to justify the effort. And with the Staff of World Tree, Lorna didn't need to worry about running out of MP.

"Heh... Heh-heh-heh-heh... It's like there's money growing right out of the ground..."

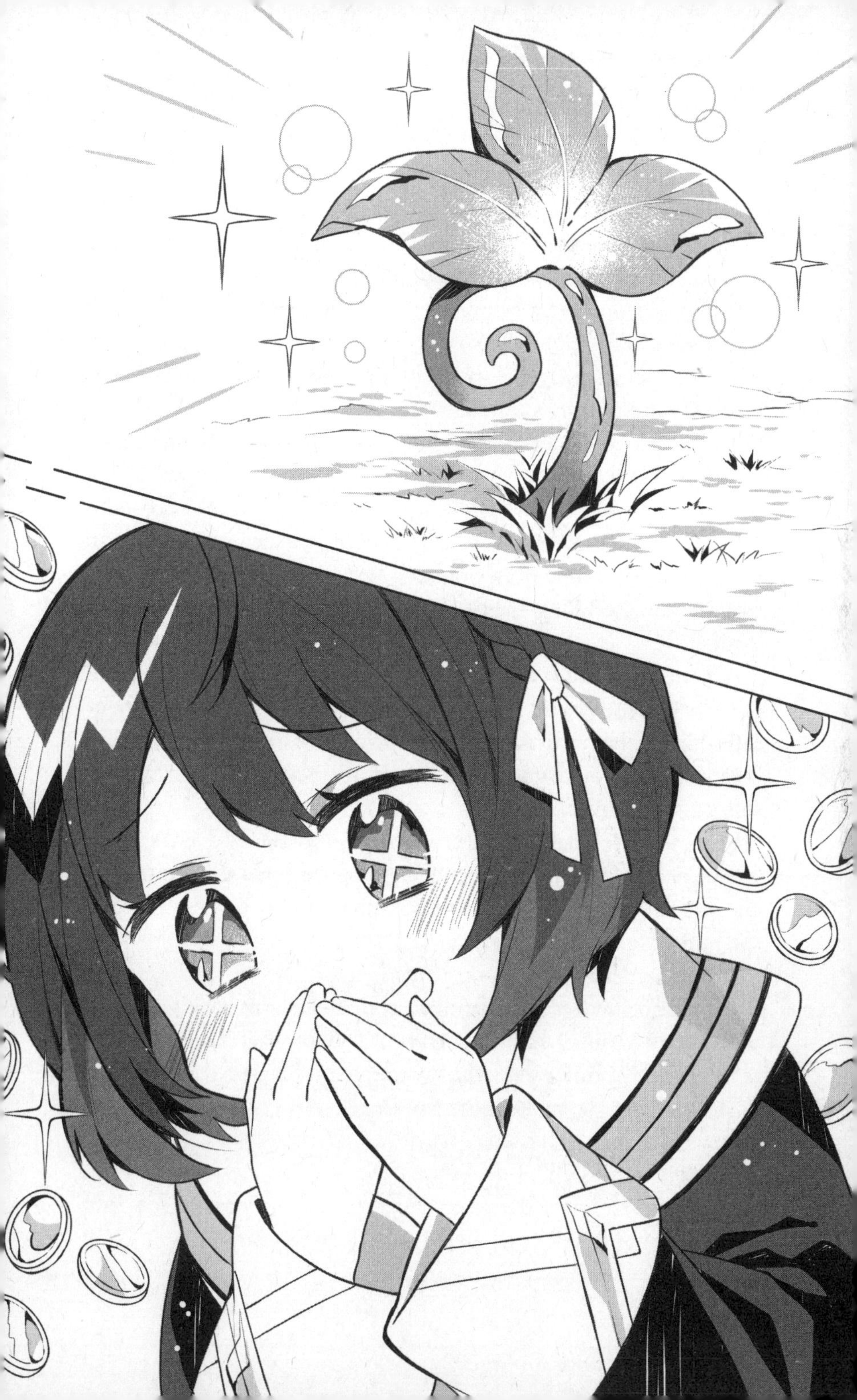

Lorna couldn't stop giggling. There were practically dollar signs in her eyes.

She spent the next few hours collecting countless Phantom Leafs.

"Woo-hoo, talk about a big haul! ♪"

Lorna was positively beaming as she checked her item list and read *Phantom Leaf x1,000*.

"If one Phantom Leaf is worth fifty thousand shil, then... I now have fifty million shil's worth!"

The work had exhausted her, but with gains like that, it had all been worth it.

I just made fifty million shil in a single day... Heh...heh-heh-heh-heh...

Initially, she'd only been hoping to make enough to get her out from under the Guugelheits' thumb. But now she was absolutely loaded.

According to the wiki, selling them all at once would lower the herbs' value. But thanks to her Item Box, Lorna could keep them safe and sell them a little at a time to avoid flooding the market.

"I guess I should go cash some of these in," she said with a self-satisfied smile.

She cast Enchanted Wings and flew into the sky, charting a course back to town. As she did, she popped open the internet to check if she was heading in the right direction. And that was when she noticed something.

"Hmm... What's this marker here?"

Directly below her was a familiar icon. She'd last seen it when she was entering Aiphoné for the first time. As for what it meant...

"Doesn't this thing show the starting point for a side quest?"

The moment she spoke those words...

"Aaaaaaaaahhhh!!!"

...a piercing shriek burst up through the forest canopy.

Chapter 9: I Gathered an Infinite Number of Herbs!

◇

Somewhere inside the Ipple Woods, Elna, princess of the elves, was running from a pack of Forest Wolves.

"Huff... H-hngh... Urk...!"

She was usually careful to avoid spots where monsters were known to gather. But on that day, the elven princess was in a hurry and failed to realize how deep into the woods she had wandered. It didn't help that the Lord of the Woods had suddenly disappeared. And though the elven people were used to walking through the forest, Elna was still just a child.

The wolves were slowly gaining on her when...

"Ah...?!"

...her foot caught the root of a tree, and she fell to the ground. She glanced back in terror as the pack of Forest Wolves descended upon her.

"L-leave me alone...!"

Elna pulled out a small knife and pointed it at the wolves, but it did little to keep them at bay. They hunkered down, ready to pounce on her at any moment.

Ngh... I practiced all that magic, yet I...

Faced with a pack of monsters, Elna froze up and wasn't able to fight back. Even if she managed to activate her magic, she wasn't calm enough to focus it into a spell.

Is...is this how I die? I wasn't able to find the Phantom Leaf... And I couldn't help Mother...

How had it come to this? Until a short while ago, Elna had lived a peaceful life. But somewhere along the way, everything had fallen apart.

"Please... God... Help me!"

Just as Elna closed her eyes in prayer, she heard a voice from above.

"Petit Ice!"

* * *

The next instant—

"...?!"

Fwoooooosh!!!

—an intense blast of cold air blew through the woods, and all the wolves fell silent.

"Wh-what hap—?"

Elna nervously opened her eyes and was struck speechless.

Everything in front of her was now a mass of frosty white ice. The wolves had disappeared, and in their place were wolf-shaped ice statues, their faces twisted in terror.

"Wh-what...?"

Elna couldn't comprehend what she was seeing. This wasn't the work of an earthly being. It was more like a divine miracle...

"...!"

Suddenly, Elna felt a presence above her and raised her eyes to see what it was.

A godlike girl floated above her on wings of light. One glance was all it took for Elna to sense the enormous amount of mana radiating out from the floating figure. There was no mistaking it...

"God...! Is that you...?"

"Huh? Um, nope," responded the girl, scratching her head in confusion.

"Oh, pardon me! You must be the Savior!"

"No, no. You've got it all wrong."

Oh, I see. She's being humble.

But Elna knew the truth. One look at the item in the girl's hands told the princess all she needed to know.

That's it... The staff of legend.

The Staff of World Tree.

* * *

Elven legends told of a legendary staff. It was said that when calamity befell the land, a chosen one would take up that staff and become the Savior. And that could mean only one thing: This winged girl, she was...

"The gods must have heard my prayers and sent you here to help me!" Elna exclaimed.

"Wha—? The gods...? Well, I mean, I guess I can see how you'd come to that conclusion, but..."

"I knew it!" said Elna, tears in her eyes. She said a prayer of thanks to the winged one. "Please, O Savior! You must save my mother... You must save my village!"

"Huh...? Um, okay."

The winged girl, for her part, was bewildered by Elna's supplications.

Wh-what have I gotten myself into...?

All Lorna had been trying to do was check out the side quest marker she'd seen on the map. But in doing so, she'd gotten caught up in some kind of major incident and was now being revered as a savior by some elven girl.

She scratched her cheek and popped open the internet to see what all this was about.

■ **Side quest: The Toxic Ambitions of Dr. Zariché**
Recommended Level: 50
Activation Conditions: Defeat the Lord of the Woods
Location: Ipple Woods—Area 10
Rewards: Elf Queen's Amulet (A), free access to the Hidden Village of the Elves
◇ **Details:** Meet Princess Elna and accompany her to the Hidden Village of the Elves to get to the bottom of the mysterious illness that has overtaken her people.

This side quest contains a host of enemies that attack using status ailments, so it's recommended that you bring along items like the Antidote Necklace or a Substitute Doll. Fire-based skills come in very handy on this side quest.

Is it...too late for me to cancel this quest...?
Lorna looked at Elna, whose eyes were sparkling, and sighed in resignation.

Chapter 10   I Went to the Elven Village!

"Savior! This is the way to the Hidden Village of the Elves!"

"R-right. And could you stop calling me that?"

Shortly after she'd saved a young elven girl named Elna, Lorna found herself being pulled by the hand into the depths of the woods.

"Make sure you hold on tightly! If you don't, you'll get lost and never find your way home."

"Wh-what?! That's *really* scary!"

As they walked, the fog grew thicker and thicker until Lorna could no longer see the path ahead.

Now that I think about it... This area is called the Woods of Confusion, right?

Lorna recalled hearing tales of this place back when she lived at her family's estate. According to Elna, the fog of confusion was a barrier put up by the elves to prevent their village from being found by outsiders.

...I don't want to get lost forever.

Terrified, Lorna let herself be dragged through the spooky woods. A while later, Elna spoke up.

"We're almost at the village."

"Oh... Thank goodness," said Lorna, exhaling.

But her relief was short-lived.

*   *   *

"Begone, human!"

"Um, what?"

Lorna looked up and saw countless arrows poking out from the fog, ready to be fired. It was a group of elves.

"Wh-what are you doing?! This human is good!" Elna stepped out in front of Lorna and spread her arms wide to protect her.

"...It's Princess Elna! Filthy human! What do you plan to do with our princess?!"

The elves seemed particularly on edge. Their eyes, full of fear, were trained on Lorna.

"U-um, well... To be honest with you, I kinda just let her drag me here. I wasn't really planning on doing anything. Look, she's perfectly safe—"

"L-liar!" cried one of the elves.

"You think you can fool us? We know you're the one behind the cataclysm that's befallen the forest!"

"......"

Lorna realized the elves had plenty of reason to be suspicious of her. She had scorched the shrubbery, frozen the foliage, and torn the forest apart with tornadoes. At this point, she should have expected the elves to declare war on her.

"Th-the mana this human exudes...i-it's... Urp... *Bleeeeeeergh.*"

"H-hey, you all right? C'mon, speak to me!"

"Eek! Yaaaargh! S-s-stay away from me!!!"

"Idiot, what are you thinking, firing on her?! The princess is right— W-wait, the arrow just bounced off her!"

"H-her skin is like stone! She's a monster!"

"Curses! You damned Calamity Witch! Do you plan to destroy our forest?!"

"It seems we've no choice but to go to war with humankind, after all…!"

…This was a disaster.

All Lorna had done was stand there. And yet somehow, things were going downhill fast.

Th-this is really getting out of hand…

All she had wanted to do was collect some herbs from the woods.

I want to go back to town… I just want to trade these herbs in for some money…

Lorna gazed into the distance and thought about how badly she wanted to be anywhere but here.

"Calm yourselves!"

Elna's appeal silenced the other elves. It was a gesture befitting of a princess. Despite her childlike appearance, she had the dignified air of royalty.

"Everyone… Please settle down and behold the item in the Savior's hand."

Elna pointed at the staff Lorna was holding. The other elves looked closely and began to murmur.

"I-it cannot be. The staff of legend… The mythical Staff of World Tree?!"

Um… Is that right?

"Then, this can only mean one thing… That *you* are the Savior from our prophecies!"

Um… Are you sure?

"That is correct! Just as crisis has befallen our village, the Savior has appeared to help us!"

Um… Well, I guess.

For some reason, Elna had a smug grin.

"I-is this true…?!" said one of the elves.

"You'll save our village...?!"

"Then what we have done is an unforgivable affront to the Savior...!"

The elves all looked to Lorna, their faces twisted in a mix of confusion and awe. And all at once...

""""Please forgive us, O Savior!!!""""

...they apologized to her.

Lorna gazed at the elves, only one thought on her mind: *I...really want to go home.*

A short while later, Elna guided Lorna into the Hidden Village of the Elves.

"Whoa..."

It was a peaceful village gently lit by rays of sunlight filtering through the forest canopy. Simple houses had been built within the branches of the trees, connected by rope ladders and bridges running between them.

Lorna couldn't help but gasp in admiration. The atmosphere here was so different from Aiphoné. Something about the scene before her tickled her tourist bone in a way she hadn't yet experienced.

"This place is really pretty!" she said.

"I'm so glad to hear you say that, O Savior!"

"Um, I'm not this savior person, so please..."

Elna was acting as Lorna's tour guide, and Lorna's praise had filled her with pride. That was all well and good, of course, but...

"......"

...when Lorna looked down at the ground below, she saw countless elves kneeling in a neat line. These were the same elven soldiers who had attacked her not long ago.

*　*　*

""""Welcome to our village, O Savior of the land!"""""

"......"

Playing the tourist was starting to seem like more trouble than it was worth. Lorna felt the urge to get out of here as soon as possible well up inside her, but she resisted it.

Seeing that it was causing a commotion, Lorna had sent her Staff of World Tree to the Item Box. Thankfully, with it gone, the elves had stopped vomiting and going into a frenzy whenever she passed. But the act of putting away the staff had caused its own share of headaches.

"She's destroyed the Staff of World Tree!"
"Gyaaaaah! She really is a Calamity Witch!!!"

But more than any of that, there was something Lorna was curious about.

"What is all this...?" she asked.

As they continued deeper into the village, she'd spotted a number of elves slumped on the ground in tattered clothing. They were gaunt and moaning, "Medicine... Where's the medicine...?"

"Oh, right," she continued after a moment. "You said there was a mysterious illness sweeping through town, didn't you?"

"What? I haven't told you about the illness yet... I'm surprised to hear you know of it."

"O-oh, really? I thought I remembered you mentioning it."

It was then that Lorna recalled she had learned about the illness from the internet. She didn't know much about it, but it looked quite grave indeed. This must have been what the elves meant when they said that a crisis had befallen their village.

Hmm, I'd love to help them out, but...this doesn't seem like the kind of thing I can do much about. It's not like I'm a real savior or anything. I guess I might be able to find something about it on the internet.

As she pondered the elves' predicament, Lorna popped open the internet to look up more details on the village.

■ **Map: Hidden Village of the Elves**
A village of elves within the Ipple Woods. The village can be entered after accepting the side quest, *The Toxic Ambitions of Dr. Zariché*.
Many items can only be found in this village. The Elven Garb and Elven Nostrum, in particular, prove useful for much of the game.
If visited before clearing part one of the main story, it's possible to gain hints about how to obtain the Staff of World Tree.
Its regional delicacies are Elf juice and Elf crackers.

"...Huh. How about that."
At the very least, she now knew about the village's delicacies. She was feeling a bit peckish and hoped to find something to eat. But as she looked around, she couldn't see anything resembling a food stall.
"U-um, sorry, but uh... Is there anyplace around here where I can buy Elf juice and Elf crackers?"
"...I'm sorry. Currently, the illness has us all far too preoccupied to make either of them."
"......"
Lorna could no longer abide this mysterious illness. It was unforgivable for such a thing to stand in the way of a tourist's urge to sample the local foods.
"Elna. I swear I'll rid your village of this illness."
"Th-thank you so much! Oh, I just knew you were pure of heart, O Savior. You have my undying gratitude!"
"Hmm? Oh. Um, right."
Looking down at the elf princess, her eyes sparkling in gratitude

and admiration, Lorna found it difficult to come clean about her ulterior motives.

After this exchange, they continued their tour. And after a while, Elna gestured toward a building in front of them.

"We've arrived, O Savior! This is my home!" she said.

Wow, yep. That is one heck of a castle.

It was an enormous palace built from wood atop a gargantuan tree.

"Mother, I've brought the Savior with me."

"...Enter."

With those words, Lorna was ushered into the queen's bedroom.

A carpet embroidered with a traditional elven pattern was spread across the ground. The walls and ceiling were made of woven branches, leaving gaps through which Lorna could see the sky.

And there, in the very center of the room, was Ellhar, Queen of the Elves. She was lying on a large canopy bed. Another elf in a white robe like a doctor's stood by her bedside.

Th-this is...the elven queen?

Lorna let out an astonished gasp.

The queen exuded a mysterious beauty that transcended human understanding. Her face was pale and gaunt from illness, yet she retained a quiet dignity. Lorna had met countless nobles in her time, but she had never seen one as majestic as the queen of the elves.

"So you... You are the Savior...?" the queen asked.

"Huh? Oh... Um, yes. Th-that's me. My name is Lorna."

"I see... You have traveled far to see us, O Savior. I regret that you find me in this state."

"I-it's fine... No problem at all."

"Hmm, strange... Ah yes...," the elf queen said, turning her gaze on Lorna as though appraising her. "You are not currently in possession of the Staff of World Tree. And yet...I sense the essence of the world—a certain divinity—emanating from your person."

"...!"

The elf queen's eyes seemed to be trained directly in front of Lorna—on the internet screen she currently had open. This was a surprise—Lorna had the window in incognito mode. No one but her should have been able to see it. Perhaps the queen had sensed the internet's presence on a more instinctual level.

"Hmm-hmm... Today is a joyous day, indeed. How can I allow myself to lie here at such an auspicious time? I should—*cough, cough!*"

"M-Mother?!" cried Elna.

The queen began to cough violently, and the doctor at her bedside quickly reached out to rub her upper back.

"You should take care not to speak so much, Your Majesty... Please, take your medicine."

"A-ah... Thank you, Zariché."

The doctor, Zariché, gave the queen a vial of liquid medicine. Soon after, the queen's coughing fit came to an end, and she regained her composure.

"...Your medicine is always so effective. You, too, have done much to earn your title of savior, Zariché."

"You humble me with your kind words, Your Majesty. However, *the true Savior* would surely find a cure for this terrible illness."

Zariché spoke with a sour tone, casting a suspicious gaze in Lorna's direction. Lorna wondered if the elf saw her as a con woman here to steal her job.

"The Savior has only just arrived in our village," said the queen. "We must not ask so much of her. Besides, this strange illness ravaging our home is the worst malady to ever befall the elves."

"...Ah! B-beg your pardon, Your Majesty," apologized Zariché,

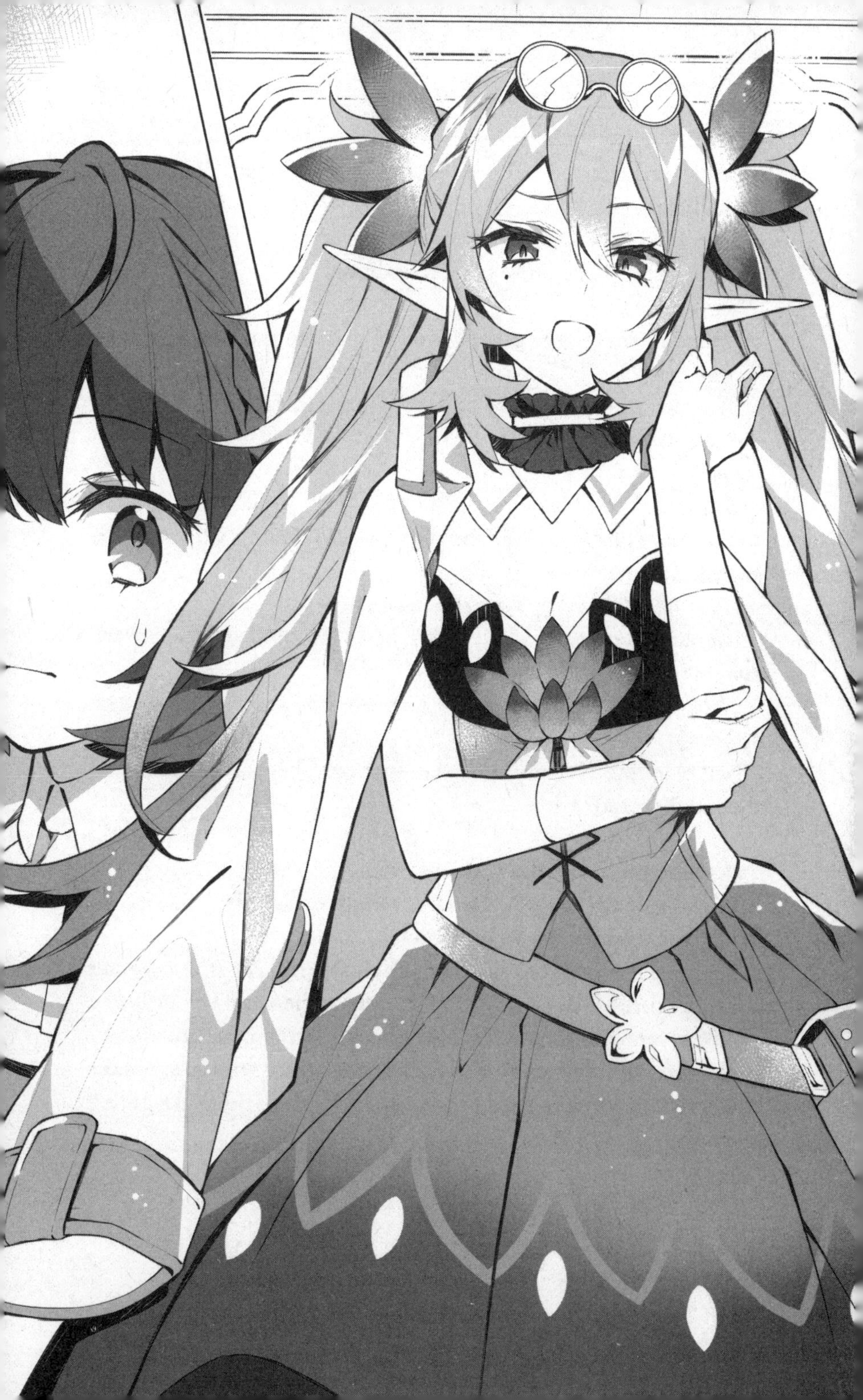

looking embarrassed. The queen's reprimand had silenced her immediately.

Then Elna nervously turned toward the doctor and asked, "T-tell me, Zariché... What of Mother's condition?"

"I'm afraid I..."

"There is no need, Zariché," said the queen with a grave nod. "Speak freely."

"In truth...Her Majesty's condition is anything but favorable. If only we had some Phantom Leafs, I would be able to prepare Elven Nostrum..."

"I...see..."

A gloomy hush fell over the room. Lorna stood there amid the awkward silence.

Uh... I kind of feel like I don't belong here...

Lorna wanted to disappear, and she quietly shuffled herself to the farthest corner of the room.

Hold on a sec... I feel like I've heard the name Zariché somewhere before...

Not thinking much of it, Lorna searched the woman's name on the internet, and...

■ **Character: Zariché Venomgarden**

A boss appearing in the Hidden Village of the Elves side quest, The Toxic Ambitions of Dr. Zariché.

Under the orders of the Guugelheit family, Zariché uses her Plant Control skill to spread poisonous pollen and wreak havoc on the elven village, selling their special nostrum for profit.

Her greatest ambition is global domination, which she plans to accomplish by enslaving the people of the world using pollen from the Queen's Heart Rose.

Oh... Okay, then... Looks like I know it all now...

Chapter 10: I Went to the Elven Village! 137

Lorna felt like she might have learned a little too much. She'd pretty much spoiled these people's whole story.

"I beg your leave, Your Majesty," said Zariché. "I must attend to my other patients."

"Yes, of course. I entrust my people to you."

"I will do my utmost," replied the doctor, lying through her teeth before leaving the queen's chambers.

As soon as she stepped outside, Lorna saw countless hands shoot out to greet her, begging for her help.

"Nngghh... Mistress Zariché!"

"Medicine, please... My daughter... She's taken a turn for the worst...!"

"Take my family's heirlooms, take anything...! But please, the medicine...!"

"Eee-hee-hee. ♡ Please give me a little time. I'll bring the medicine at the usual hour."

Hearing that, the throng of elves cried out in joy. Zariché was beloved by the people of the village. They didn't have the slightest inkling that she was the source of their strange illness.

Back in the queen's chambers, a terrible hush had fallen over mother and daughter.

"Elna...I'm afraid I don't have much time left in this world."

Elna looked up in shock at the queen's words. "B-but, Mother! S-surely you'll be well in no time. The Savior is finally here, and—"

"I'm afraid it's too late. I know more than anyone how dire my condition has become... If only we could procure the mythical Phantom Leaf, then...perhaps we might be able to brew Elven Nostrum. However—*cough, cough*."

"M-Mother! Please, you mustn't speak!"

"Ah, how regrettable... Were I to be granted but a single wish...I would have loved nothing more than...to see the Savior...d-deliver the world from...dark...ness..."

"Mother?! No...! M-Motheeer!"

Lorna, having been present for the unfolding drama, hesitantly raised a hand.

"................Um, e-excuse me."

She was hesitant to say something so ridiculous at such a solemn time, but she felt she could no longer stay silent.

"If you need Phantom Leaf, I, uh, have a thousand of them. Do you...want some?"

""...What?""

All of a sudden, dozens of herbs began to emerge from Lorna's hand. *Pop, pop, pop.* They were all Phantom Leafs, a medicinal herb that had only been seen a handful of times throughout history.

"Oh, and another thing. If you're curious about the source of the illness: It's caused by poisonous pollen that Zariché person has been spreading around the village. So if you deal with her, that should stop the illness from spreading."

"""................................"""

The queen and princess of the elves froze, their mouths agape.

Lorna felt like she'd totally ruined the mood. And that wasn't all.

Sorry, Zariché, she thought earnestly. *I might have just destroyed your ambitions, too.*

Chapter 11　I Tried Making Elven Nostrum!

"How are things going on your end, Zariché?"

"Exceedingly well, Margrave! By your leave, I've been able to make quite an impressive profit. ♡ And everything is proceeding as planned. ♡"

Somewhere in the hidden village of the elves, Zariché Venomgarden was sitting at a tea table surrounded by poisonous-looking plants, in a large greenhouse that resembled a palace. She had thrown her white doctor's gown to one side and was gracefully sipping her tea, a deep-purple concoction.

The voice coming from the communications crystal placed on the table before her belonged to none other than Margrave Guugelheit.

"I must say, that pollen you control certainly is something."

"Yes, indeed. There is no defense against my poisonous pollen. ♡ It is both colorless and odorless, and once dispersed through the air, it is impossible to avoid breathing it in. ♡ And when the conditions are just so, I can spread the pollen for hundreds of miles in every direction. ♡"

Zariché cast her gaze around the greenhouse. The plant monsters she had raised emitted a noxious purple pollen that filled the air like a poisonous gas. This pollen would slowly sap the strength from anyone who inhaled it. She'd initially started spreading it just to see what would happen, and…

My experiment was a huge success! ♡

Zariché scooped countless jewels up into her hands, entranced.

Only the medicine she made could relieve the symptoms of those suffering from the pollen, and only temporarily. As a result, the elves in the village depended on her just to make it through the day. At this point, they toiled only to afford medicine—and handed all their wealth over to Zariché.

But unbeknownst to them, the grim truth was that their money went right back into raising more noxious plants to spread more poisonous pollen.

"None of this would have been possible without the funding and mana you provide me. ♡ I have no doubt that my pollen will benefit you as well, Margrave Guugelheit. ♡ "

"I-indeed. And so… Well… About that mana…"

"…Is something the matter, Margrave?"

"A-ah, n-no. Everything is fine… Please, keep up the good work. At this point, your plan is our only means to— Er, *cough, cough, cough*. In any event, that is all!"

"Hmm…?"

The margrave's mumbling worried Zariché somewhat, but if everything was proceeding according to plan, then surely there would be no problem.

"…Understood! ♡ All that I do, I do for you, Margrave Guugelheit! ♡ "

Soon after Zariché ended her communication, she burst into uncontrollable laughter.

"…Hee-hee… Eee-hee-hee! ♡ Eeeee-hee-hee-hee-hee! ♡♡♡ "

She had completely dropped her doctor act. Grinning like a fool, she cruelly mocked the world around her.

"Ahhh! ♡ Those precious, precious fools! ♡ Do those stuck-up nobles really think that *they* control *me*? ♡ *I'm* the only one in the entire world who can control this pollen! ♡ "

Zarich́é turned to gaze at a massive thorny stem growing in the center of the greenhouse. At its crown sprouted a single purple bud. This was Zariché's secret weapon, which not even the Guugelheits knew about. The ultimate flower...

The Queen's Heart Rose.

The moment the flower blossomed, Zariché would become queen of the world. The great elf queen, the proud Guugelheit family—all of them would become her servants.

"Eee-hee-hee. ♡ This is only the beginning. ♡ First, I will take the elven throne for myself. And then—the world! I'll become queen of it all! ♡ "

World domination—for years and years, that had been Zariché's sole ambition. It was why she'd made a pact with outsiders and why she'd made the elves suffer.

And it had all been worth it—her preparations were almost complete. Soon, the Queen's Heart Rose would blossom. But first...

"Oh dear, oh dear. ♡ I almost forgot—it's time for everyone's medicine. ♡ My, my, the work of a *Savior* is never done! ♡ "

Zariché cackled as she donned her white doctor's gown. Then she grabbed her medicine box and left the greenhouse.

Countless elves were surely waiting for her medicine. They knew nothing of her ambitions. They had even called her their savior. They offered her everything they had for a taste of her medicine.

Watching them beg was Zariché's favorite time of day. That day, too, she would indulge herself with their supplications. Or so she'd thought.

".........What?"

The moment Zariché stepped out of her greenhouse, she was met with an unbelievable sight.

"Cheeeers!"
"Thank you, O Savior!"

"All hail the true Savior!"

"Drink, drink as much as you want! We'll never pay for that absurdly expensive medicine again!"

The elves of the village were throwing a big party. Everyone was holding wooden tankards full of liquid and cheerfully celebrating.

Wh-wh-wh...whaaaaaaaaaaat?!

There was no way anyone who had inhaled her poisonous pollen could be moving so freely and vigorously. No one knew that better than Zariché, for she had designed it herself.

Wh-what is all this...?!

A panicked Zariché pushed her way through the crowd of elves. And standing in the middle of that crowd, she found...

Th-that child...?!

It was the same absent-minded-looking girl Zariché had seen earlier in the queen's bedroom.

Back when Zariché first spotted her, the girl had about as much presence as a gaseous vapor. Now, however, she wore a sash emblazoned with the word *savior* and scratched her head bashfully as the other elves doted on her. In front of her was a cauldron full of bubbling green liquid.

"There is still plenty of medicine to go around! We have enough for everyone, so step forward! Don't be shy!"

"Let us toast to the recovery of our people," called the elven queen, "and to the Savior who has blessed our village with her presence! Come, everyone! Drink! Be merry!"

""""Hip, hip, hooray!""""

The one pouring this supposed medicine into the elves' cups was none other than Princess Elna. And standing beside her, looking healthy as could be, was Queen Ellhar.

Medicine...?! Don't tell me—!

Zariché suddenly realized what the elves had in their tankards—they were imbibing *Elven Nostrum*.

Wh-wh-wh...whaaaaaaaaaaat?!

Despite her ruse, Zariché was a doctor of the apothecarial arts. She knew better than anyone that brewing such a large batch of Elven Nostrum was unthinkable. Its main ingredient, Phantom Leaf, was far too rare.

Zariché was unable to process the situation.

Why...?! Why, why, why, why, why, whyyyyy?! Th-this makes no sense! My...my plan! It was impeccable in every way! Earlier this very day, everyone was sick with my poison. They treated me as their Savior. And now...!

What could have happened to change the situation so drastically in only a few short hours? The scene before her was so incomprehensible that Zariché thought she was having a nightmare.

That girl they call the Savior... She can't possibly have...? No! Impossible. Inconceivable! She's nothing but a weak little girl. She didn't even come bearing the symbol of the Savior, the Staff of World Tree. I was certain Princess Elna had simply found some human apothecary...

A flurry of thoughts rushed through Zariché's mind. And before she knew it, all the elves' gazes were trained on her.

Wh-what is this...?

Their expressions were not the usual ones of respect and admiration. Their eyes, aimed straight at Zariché, were full of rage and resentment.

"Hey... She's here. The one who poisoned us."

"She made us all sick using her pollen, right?"

"I thought something was off about the whole thing. She came up with medicine for the illness awfully quick..."

"Create the problem and sell the solution, huh...?"

"This con artist robbed us of our fortunes..."

*   *   *

The elves continued to murmur among themselves.

It seemed the nostrum was the least of Zariché's worries. Her plan had been laid bare.

H-how...?! Hoooooowwwww?!

Too many things were happening all at once. Zariché thought she would go mad.

But this was no time to fall into confusion. Looking around, she realized that the elves had pointed their bows and staves directly at her. Staying any longer would be dangerous.

"Ngh! Dammit!"

She smashed a vial against the ground, and with a *poof*, a smoke screen enveloped the area. The smoke, which was filled with a paralyzing pollen, brought the elves to their knees.

"Guh... Can't...move...!"

"It's just as the Savior said! She's the one who caused the illness!"

"That no-good— Where'd she go?!"

"Search the area! We can't allow her to escape!"

"Eee...eeeek...!"

Zariché, her face twisted in fear, made a panicked dash for the greenhouse. In her rush, she flung her medicine box to the ground and ripped off the white robe she was wearing so quickly that it tore.

Meanwhile, Lorna had been standing by watching the commotion.

"Are you certain we should allow Zariché to escape...?" the queen asked with some concern.

"Yes," Lorna said casually. "We don't have what we need to deal with her just yet."

It would be great if the elves managed to apprehend her, but… according to the internet, defeating Zariché without some means of preventing status ailments would be no easy task. Worse, if cornered, she might unleash her trump card.

And so the elves gave up pursuit, just as Lorna had instructed. Instead, they set about putting her plan into action.

"This plan of yours… It involves the nostrum?" asked the queen.

"In a way, yes." Lorna continued to stir the cauldron of Elven Nostrum as she answered.

"We've more nostrum than we could possibly need… Are you certain you should be using so much MP?"

"Don't worry about that. I've got plenty left. Besides, I should be just about done."

"…?"

At that very moment, something happened.

SKILL UP! Alchemy IV ➔ Alchemy V
Accessories can now be crafted with Alchemy!

"Okay, ready! ♪"

The words Lorna had been waiting for appeared before her eyes.

It had worked just as the internet said it would: To level one's Alchemy skill, all one had to do was continue to use their MP on Alchemy.

Luckily, Lorna had a practically limitless pool of MP to draw from, and Elven Nostrum required a ton of it to craft. It was essentially the perfect environment for boosting her level.

And now… we finally have a way to deal with status ailments.

Alchemy V enabled Lorna to craft accessories. And apparently, those accessories were necessary to safely battle Zariché.

Lorna threw a bunch of cloth and cotton—the necessary crafting ingredients—into the cauldron.

"Alchemy!"

Then—*poof*—a puff of smoke shot up from the cauldron.

"Wha—?!"

Pop, pop, pop, pop, pop!

Countless stuffed dolls began to appear.

The alchemical recipe Lorna found on the internet had been a success—she had crafted Substitute Dolls.

■ **Equipment (Accessories): Substitute Doll**
Rank: F
Type: Accessory
Price: 2,000 shil
Effect: Takes damage for the user a single time (Substitute Doll is destroyed after one use).

◊ Details: Despite its low rank, the Substitute Doll is a very broken accessory.

Its most famous application is trivializing the side quest, *The Toxic Ambitions of Dr. Zariché*. But with effective equip swapping, this accessory is incredibly useful for even Hard mode bosses.

Also, despite the in-game description stating that the doll takes damage for the user only a single time...

Apparently, these things were really good for dealing with Zariché. But something about them bothered Lorna...

"Uh... Why do these things look like *me*?"

For whatever reason, the Substitute Dolls had come out of the cauldron looking like tiny cartoonish versions of Lorna. Without realizing it, she had created an army of Lorna plushies.

"Oh my goodness! Stuffed Saviors! They're...they're...simply *adorable*!"

"U-um... You really think so?"

Elna seemed to love the dolls.

G-great. Now I'm some kind of weirdo who crafted a bunch of dolls in her own likeness...

Lorna didn't know how to feel about this turn of events.

"Savior, what of these dolls...?" asked the queen.

"Um, well... These are called Substitute Dolls. They're equipment that takes damage in your place... I guess they're kind of like amulets of protection... If you wear one, it'll keep you safe from the poisonous pollen. So please, hand them out to everyone."

"These Savior dolls... Are they truly capable of something so miraculous...? O Savior! You're incredible!"

"Hmm, I see... They must be sacred icons. We must enshrine them at once!"

"Um, actually, if you don't equip them, they won't do anything," said Lorna.

"But if we do that, they will take the brunt of any assault and be ruined!"

"Right, but that's *what they're for*. Get it?"

This group of elves were intent on wasting time worshipping the dolls. But they weren't the only ones who seemed to have misunderstood.

"Wha—? Whoa! I knocked over the pot of stew, look out!"

"Oh no! The Savior dolls! They'll be ruined by the hot stew!"

"I won't let that happen! *Hup!* Gyaaaaaaaah!"

For some reason, another group of elves was putting themselves in harm's way to protect the dolls.

"You're... You've got it all backward..."

This nonsense was beginning to give Lorna a headache. But whatever the case, her preparations were now complete.

"All right, well, I'm going to head off for a little bit. Oh, and don't stop the party on my account."

"...Wherever are you going, O Savior?"
"I'm just gonna go put an end to Zariché's ambitions."

""............Huh?""

And so Lorna headed for Zariché's greenhouse, humming a little tune as she went.

Chapter 12 I Put an End to the Bad Guy's Ambitions!

"*Huff... Huff...* I should be safe inside the greenhouse..."

Meanwhile, Zariché had done what she could to lose the elves chasing her and had escaped back to her glass lair.

But when she looked outside, she saw that the other elves were gathering around the greenhouse in droves. They were hunting her down like a heretical witch.

Wh-what is going on here...?

Only a few hours prior, she had been revered as the village's Savior. This had all happened so suddenly—there had been no warning sign that things were about to fall apart. Unless...

...That girl. This all started when she showed up.

The girl the elves now heralded as their Savior.

From the moment she'd shown up, the entire situation had been turned on its head at an unfathomable speed. In a few short hours, a massive batch of Elven Nostrum had been brewed, Zariché's plan had been laid bare, and the entire village had lost their trust in her. All that dependency she'd carefully built up—years of planning, undone in an instant.

Wh-what is she...? She couldn't possibly be the true Savior...could she?

Zariché felt pursued by some unknowable monster. Her body began to tremble.

If Margrave Guugelheit were to find out what I've allowed to happen, I'd—

And just as she thought those words...

"Zariché! Come in, Zariché. Is something the matter?"

"...M-Margrave Guugelheit?!"

...the margrave's voice called out from the communications crystal at the worst possible time.

"You seem flustered... Is there a problem?"

"N-n-n-no! No problem at all! None whatsoever! Everything here is proceeding perfectly!"

"Excellent, excellent. There have been reports of all manner of mysterious natural disasters lately, after all. Now, ahem... Well, you see... There was something I forgot to mention earlier—"

"O-oh, dear! I am so terribly sorry! It seems something's come up and I have to run. Let's talk later!"

"Uh? Wai—"

Zariché ended the communication from her side.

Bad, bad, bad... This is so very, very bad...!

If the Guugelheits found out that Zariché's plans had been foiled, she would immediately lose their support. There would be no coming back from a hit like that.

"Th-then I suppose I have no choice... It's time to unleash my ultimate weapon!"

Zariché firmed her resolve and began adjusting the magical implements in her greenhouse. The next moment—*wooooooom!*—all the mana flowing through the space began to gather at the center of the room, inside the massive rose.

"E-everything's still fine... It may not be complete, but no one knows about my secret weapon, my true ambition..."

Zariché looked up at the massive bud as it began to quiver.

Chapter 12: I Put an End to the Bad Guy's Ambitions!

The Queen's Heart Rose—a flower whose pollen had the power to bend anyone who breathed it to her will.

Once the flower had fully blossomed, it would release its pollen into the air, and everyone within a radius of several hundred miles would be inflicted with the Charm status. It wouldn't matter if they were commoner, noble, or royalty—they would all do Zariché's bidding.

Then she would command her new army of followers to spread Queen's Heart Roses across the land. Zariché's dominion would grow and grow until, finally, she would be queen of the entire world.

A few small missteps now would soon be more than made up for.

"Eee-hee-hee-hee-hee! ♡. All I need to do is buy some time so my darling Queen's Heart Rose can blossom. And then I'll have won! ♡ "

Zariché grinned triumphantly.

This greenhouse was her fortress. Its ramparts were made of thorns as strong as iron, and they gushed pollen that inflicted Poison, Sleep, Paralysis, and so on. What's more, it was guarded by poison spike–firing cacti and man-eating plants with razor-sharp fangs. Every plant in the vicinity was a monster, and thanks to her Plant Control skill, they were all soldiers at her command. The greenhouse may as well have been an impregnable dungeon.

A handful of unforeseen setbacks were no matter. Zariché still had everything under control.

"Eee-hee-hee-hee! ♡ If they think they can reach me, then let them try! ♡ "

But as Zariché cackled maniacally...

Craaaaaash!!!

...the ceiling of the greenhouse shattered.

"..........What?"

Shards of glass caught the light and sparkled as they rained down around her. Zariché looked up in shock.

What...? Are they attacking from above?

Through the rain of glittering glass shards, Zariché could just make something out. It was the silhouette of someone descending toward her, borne on wings of light. It looked like an angel.

After staring for a moment, Zariché realized the figure was holding something—the Staff of World Tree.

Um... Why is there a terrifying divine being crashing through my ceiling...?

When the figure alighted before Zariché, her face went pale. It was Lorna, just as pale-faced as she was.

Whoooooa...! thought Lorna. *That scared me half to death...! What happened? The map on the internet said there was supposed to be a "secret path" up there...*

Lorna brought up the internet again to make sure she had read it right.

■ **Map: Poison Rose Gardens**
Dungeon found within the Hidden Village of the Elves.
This dungeon is notorious for killing players on their first visit.
The droves of plant monsters littering the dungeon spread pollen that inflicts a variety of status ailments across a large area. It is likely that the unprepared will find themselves unable to act due to Paralysis or Sleep, forced to watch themselves slowly die from Poison.
If you level the exploration skill Climbing high enough beforehand, you can reach a secret path on the roof of the dungeon. This path is a shortcut that leads directly to the boss.

Lorna had followed the internet's instructions to the letter and walked out onto the glass roof of the greenhouse expecting to find a path. Much to her surprise, that had landed her here. She hadn't expected the "shortcut" to literally cut a hole in the greenhouse's ceiling.

"I... I'm still paying off the loan on this place...," muttered Zariché incredulously as she stared in horror at the shattered ceiling. But after a moment, she snapped out of her daze and turned to face Lorna.

"...Eee-hee-hee! ♡ Welcome, foolish intruder, to my garden of venom. ♡ "

Zariché, having regained her composure, lifted her skirt slightly and offered Lorna a curtsy.

Hmph... I haven't lost yet. ♡

Zariché snickered to herself. Yes, she had been taken aback—but that was all and nothing more. She had not lost her advantage.

"So you've come expecting to fight me, have you? What a shaaame. ♡ From the moment you entered my glass fortress, your fate was sealed. I win! ♡ "

"...Wh-what do you mean?" asked Lorna.

"Eee-hee-hee. ♡ You'll see soon enough. My special poisonous pollen should begin to take effect aaany moment now. ♡ "

"Huh...? Oh."

The girl must have finally realized what was happening. But it was too late.

"Even if you somehow saw through my plans...it would be impossible for you to avoid all the ailments about to befall you here in this greenhouse. ♡ Not even Elven Nostrum can save you once my paralyzing and sleep-inducing pollens have you immobilized! You wouldn't even be able to bring it to your lips! ♡ "

"Um. Right."

It didn't matter how much HP Zariché's opponents had, nor how strong they were—not once they were inundated with the pollen's countless status ailments. Unable to move from Paralysis and Sleep, the victim would slowly succumb to Poison and die. That was Zariché's invincible combat strategy.

"Eee-hee-hee-hee! ♡ Panic all you want; it's already too late. ♡ Now show me... Let me see your dance of agony! ♡ Eeeee-hee-hee-hee! ♡"

"......"

"Eee-hee-hee-hee... You'll be feeling it soon! So, so soon! Eee-hee-hee-hee-hee! ♡"

"........."

"Eee...hee... Eee-hee-hee... ♡"

"............"
"............"
"............"

"...My pollen isn't working on you, is it?"

"Um... N-no, it isn't... Sorry..."

Lorna felt bad, but she couldn't exactly tell Zariché that she'd simply looked up how to counter her status ailment–based strategy ahead of time using the internet.

The page Lorna had read told her everything she needed to know about the poisonous boss.

■ **Boss: Queen's Heart Rose & Zariché**
Spawn Location: Poison Rose Gardens
Level: 53
Weakness: Fire, Ice
Resistance: Water, Earth, Poison, Paralysis, Darkness
Rewards: Queen's Heart Thorn (80 percent), Queen's Heart Petal (50 percent), Queen's Heart Crown (20 percent)
◇ **Details: A tough boss fight full of status ailments and traps.**

The boss area is full of Toxiblooms, Paraflowers, and Doze-blossoms that inflict status ailments and need to be dealt with promptly. Moreover, this boss must be defeated before the Queen's Heart Rose in the center of the room blossoms.

Because it is only possible to protect against a limited number of status ailments at one time, players must be prepared to deal with at least some of their negative effects past the halfway point.

However, this can be circumvented completely by equipping a Substitute Doll, which renders all the boss's status ailments ineffective.

"I...can't believe this actually worked...," muttered Lorna as she stared down at the Substitute Doll.

The item's description stated that it could only prevent damage a single time. However, according to the internet, a more accurate description of the effect was this: *Substitute Doll will continue to take damage for the user until its 1 HP is depleted.*

In effect, that meant that attacks like poisonous pollen, which only inflicted status ailments and did no damage, could be intercepted by the doll an infinite number of times. A single physical strike would tear the doll to shreds, of course. But thankfully, the plant monsters were rooted to the soil and unable to move, severely limiting their attack range. And for Lorna, who was floating above the ground, avoiding the monsters' attacks was trivial.

In other words—Lorna was completely protected from the effects of Zariché's status ailments. All she had to do now was attack from a distance and secure her victory.

"Okay, let's start with—Terra Drain!"

Fwoooooooosh!!!

A massive amount of MP flowed out from the poisonous flowers and into her staff, and she put it to use right away.

"Next, a full poweeeer...Petit Ice!"

*　*　*

Lorna pointed her staff at the Queen's Heart Rose as she called out the name of her spell.

Crack-crickle-crackk!

Ice gushed forth like a massive frozen tidal wave. The frigid blast easily engulfed the Queen's Heart Rose and still had enough force left to wash over the rest of the plants in the greenhouse, freezing them all.

Queen's Heart Rose defeated! You gained 8,787 EXP!
LEVEL UP! Lv. 42 ➔ Lv. 44
Dozeblossom swarm defeated! You gained 820 EXP!
Toxibloom swarm defeated! You gained 1,260 EXP!
Paraflower swarm defeated! You gained 1,040 EXP!
You learned the Plant Killer I skill!
SKILL UP! Art of Slaughter I ➔ Art of Slaughter II
SKILL UP! Magic VII ➔ Magic VIII
You learned the Petit Bind and Petit Charge starter spells!

Obtained Title: "Queen's Heart Rose Exterminator"

"Wh-wh-wh…whaaaaaaaaat?!"

Zariché's jaw dropped. She had never seen such powerful magic, not even among the elves, who were renowned for their long history of spellcraft. She couldn't comprehend the fact that a single human had unleashed such a terrifying spell.

"Wh-what was that…? Some manner of wide-scale eradication magic…?!"

"Wide-scale what? I just used a basic starter spell."

Zariché had indeed heard the girl incant the name of a simple starter spell. In other words, this winged girl was trying to make a point…

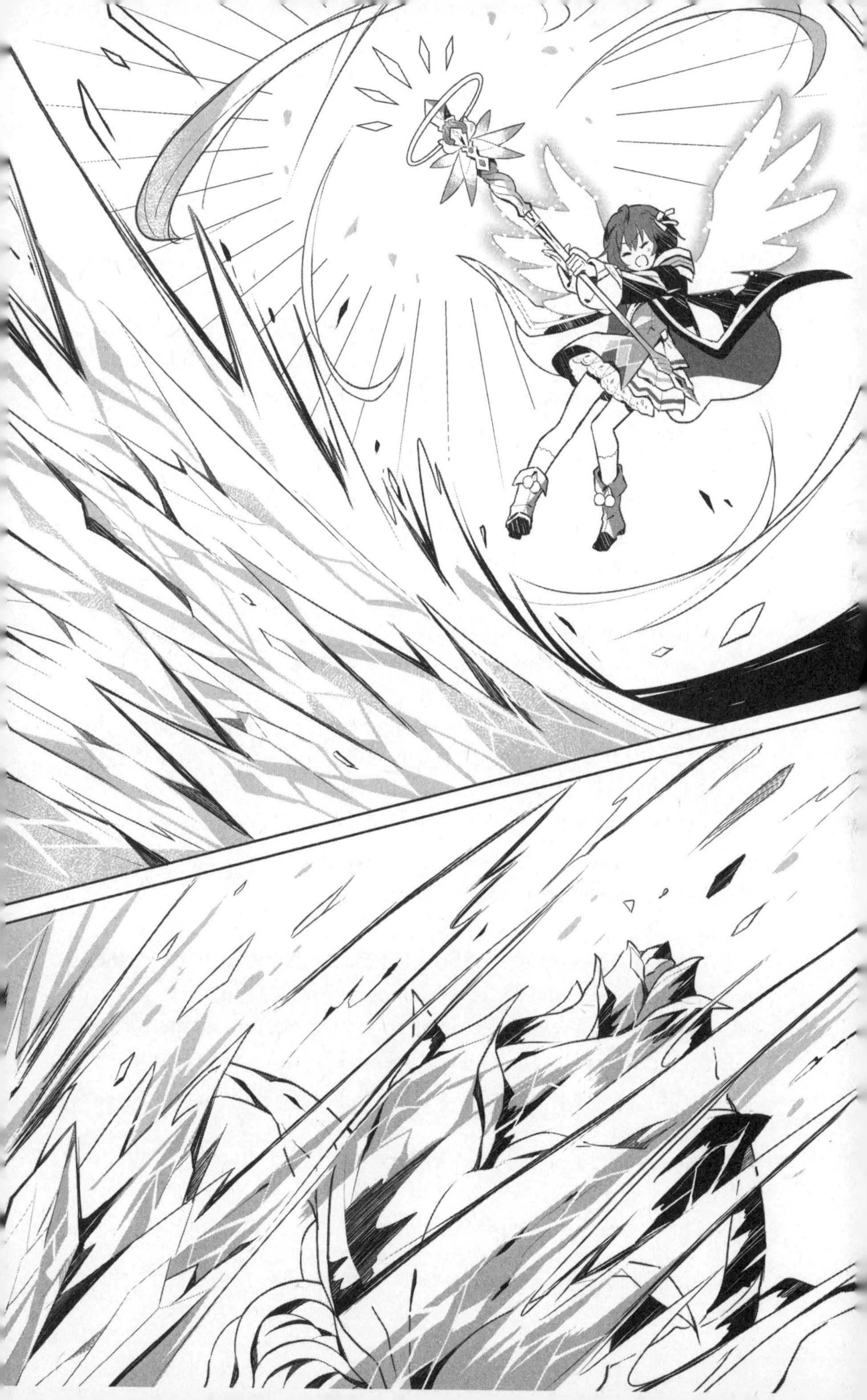

* * *

"A weak starter spell is enough to deal with the likes of you."

Whether that had been Lorna's intent was beside the point—it was true.

I... I don't understand what I'm seeing... The Queen's Heart Rose... It was defeated with a single attack...? How could this be...? My plan! It was perfect! And now... This child... How does she seem to know everything...?

Zariché's mind was blank. Nothing made any sense. But one thing was for sure: Everything she had been building up to, everything she valued, her very understanding of the world—all of it had been shattered in an instant.

Among the confusion, one thing was clear.

I... I can't win this...

The winged girl before her was strong beyond reason.

It was like she knew everything. Every move she made was impeccable. She was perfectly protected from the pollen's status ailments, and she was able to unleash spells so powerful they defied all logic.

Surely she was only *acting* like an absent-minded fool as a ploy so her opponents would let down their guard. The girl had defeated Zariché completely, through cunning and sheer power.

"Eee... Eee-hee... Eee-hee-hee... ♡"

Zariché laughed meekly. She felt broken. None of her schemes would do her any good—she could not defeat this girl.

Queen of the World—Zariché had once envisioned herself as befitting of that title. But this girl seemed far more worthy of it.

Zariché let out a long sigh, then began to speak.

"Please............please don't kill me..."

Her body trembling, the toxic doctor willingly surrendered.

Chapter 13   I Became the Savior of the World!

"...And that's about the size of it. Miss Zariché was planning to use a monster called the Queen's Heart Rose to spread pollen that would have put everyone in the world under her control. But I took care of all the plant monsters producing pollen and brought you Miss Zariché. So you don't have to worry about any of that now."

"Please don't kill me...," Zariché mumbled.

"""".............""""

Soon after saving the world from Dr. Zariché's toxic ambitions, Lorna explained everything that had (and would have) happened to the elves.

"Um. Are you all okay? You're so quiet... Don't tell me. Is there already something else troubling your village?"

"Not quite... We are simply at a loss for what to say. How shall I put this?" Ellhar, Queen of the Elves, spoke on behalf of her people.

"It all happened so fast... I have *no idea* what just happened."

In the end, Lorna handed Zariché over to the queen to decide her punishment.

Zariché, for her part, seemed to have been scared straight. And it turned out she was quite weak when she had no plant monsters to control. Taking these facts into consideration, the queen settled on indefinite forced labor under supervision, rather than sentencing her to death.

Then the elves decided to kick off a host of celebrations. They wanted to commemorate everyone's recovery, welcome the Savior, express their joy over Zariché's defeat, and toast Lorna saving the world.

And so that day in the Hidden Village of the Elves, several large parties were held in tandem.

"Woo-hoo! How long has it been since I partied like this…?"
"It was this afternoon. In fact, I don't think we ever stopped…"
"Wait, what are we celebrating again?"
"Who cares?! Drink, drink! It's a day worth celebrating, no matter what the reason!"
"Yeeeaaah! All hail Lorna the Savior!"

The elves, normally thought to be rather formal, drank and sang to their heart's content. The sounds of tankards clacking and beautiful singing voices echoed throughout the woods.

As the party continued through the night, fairies who looked like orbs of light gathered around to join in. Their glowing bodies lit the festivities in a dreamlike glow.

"Well, that was a lot. But I'm glad I was able to help," Lorna said with a contented sigh as she sipped on Elf Juice and munched on Elf crackers.

Lorna had always been weak; she'd never really had a chance to help people before. So being thanked and seeing people so happy with her was a wholly new experience. That alone had made the trip to the village worthwhile, she supposed.

As Lorna sat thinking…
"Wheeee!"

"Hey, wait up!"

...two children running around energetically slammed into her with a loud *bonk*.

"Oh! Sor—"

"Wheeee!"

"Hey, wait up!"

The children, seemingly unaware that they had bumped into someone, continued crying out joyfully as they stepped in place, still pressed against Lorna.

"Wheeee!"

"Hey, wait up!"

"......"

"Wheeee!"

"Hey, wait up!"

"......"

Lorna silently took a step backward.

Their way no longer impeded, the children resumed chasing each other around in circles.

"Wheeee!"

"Hey, wait up!"

"..............."

Lorna watched them in silent disbelief as they chased each other in a circle, around and around, on and on, and on, and on...

...*What's happening? This is super weird...*

The strange occurrence distracted Lorna completely, making her lose her train of thought. She had the sinking feeling that she had seen something she was never meant to see.

Just then...

"Are you enjoying yourself, O Savior?"

"There you are, Savior!"

"Oh, Your Majesty. Elna. Hi."

Queen Ellhar and Elna had wandered over together to check up on her.

"The villagers are more cheerful than I have ever seen them," said the queen. "All of this is thanks to you."

"Y-you really think so?"

"Of course! I just *knew* you were the Savior, O Savior!" exclaimed Elna, her eyes sparkling as she grabbed Lorna's hand. "I bet you've been on all sorts of adventures, right?! Oh, please, Savior! I want to hear tales of your travels!"

"Um..."

"I heard that only someone who has overcome *all sorts* of difficult trials is worthy of the Staff of World Tree. How did you overcome them, Savior?"

"W-well, I..."

Lorna was at a complete loss. All told, her entire journey had lasted only three days so far. And as for the staff, she had found a way to skip its trial entirely... But she couldn't find it in her heart to burst Elna's bubble.

"Ha-ha-ha. It would appear my Elna has become quite a fan, O Savior. Come now, Elna. Let us not trouble the Savior with so many questions, hmm?"

The queen seemed to sense Lorna's unease and quelled her daughter's curiosity.

"Oh... I didn't mean to be a bother," said Elna. "I'm sorry, Savior..."

"No, no... I wouldn't say you were a bother, exactly," Lorna replied.

For a brief moment, Lorna was relieved to be spared an awkward conversation.

Then again...

But after a moment, she began to reconsider. The Staff of World Tree was an important item in elven culture.

I...really don't deserve to have this staff.

Not only had she cheated to get her hands on it, but now the elves revered her as though she were a savior instead of a fraud. Lorna knew she should come clean to the elves and return the staff to them.

If I don't, I think the guilt alone might kill me…

And so with some trepidation…

"Your Majesty, Elna… I have something important to say to you."

"…What's the matter, Savior?"

…Lorna steeled her resolve and began to explain everything that had happened over the past few days.

She told them about being thrown out of the Guugelheit household, about the strange skill known as Internet, and about how that skill had allowed her to bypass the trials and obtain the staff.

She had planned to keep everything a secret, but the elves hardly left their village, and she felt that she could trust them. Besides, the pressure of keeping everything under wraps had been weighing on Lorna's conscience; she needed to get it all off her chest.

"…And that's about everything."

After Lorna wrapped up her tale, the queen and princess sat in shock for a while.

"Y-you're saying you have a skill that allows you to look upon the words of the gods? And that all the secrets of the world are written therein…? It…truly boggles the mind."

"How could those no-good meanies abandon someone as kind, strong, and cool as you, Savior? How despicable!"

"Um… What?"

Queen Ellhar seemed captivated by the details of the internet. Meanwhile, Elna had turned her frustrations on Lorna's former family.

The pair of royals had mostly ignored the main point of Lorna's tale—that she had obtained the staff through unjust means.

"Um, aren't you…y'know, angry at me?" she asked nervously.

She had expected the elves to have lost all faith in her by the time she concluded her story.

"…Hmm? Angry? What for?" asked Elna, sounding confused.

"Well, I *am* the daughter of the human Zariché was working with, so I... But more than that, I know this staff is important to your people. And I only got it because I cheated..."

The Staff of World Tree in Lorna's hands was a sacred object to the elven people, so...

"...I think it's best that I return this to you, Your Majesty."

The staff clearly belonged with the elves. As long as they kept it hidden in their village, it would be safe from anyone who might try to use it for nefarious purposes.

Lorna presented the staff to Queen Ellhar.

"".........""

The queen and the princess exchanged glances, and a moment of silent passed. Then the two of them broke out in laughter.

"To think you have been concerned with something like that all this time."

"Uh...?"

"Oh, pardon me. I simply could not help being amused that one with so much power was concerned over something so trivial."

"T-trivial...?"

"The trials themselves are of little concern. What truly matters is what you accomplish with the staff's power. The elves of this village have borne witness to your fine deeds, Lady Lorna—one of which, I must remind you, was saving the world."

"All I know is you're an amazing Savior, Lorna!"

Lorna felt tears well up in her eyes at their praise. She felt like she had received enough compliments to last her an entire lifetime. Lorna had hardly ever been praised growing up, so while she was embarrassed, she had to admit, it felt pretty nice.

"And besides," said the princess with a chuckle, "the fact that you were chosen to wield a skill that shows you the very words of the gods is proof enough that you're the true Savior."

"The Guugelheits, huh...," muttered the queen, moving on. "To think I would hear that name again."

"You know of them?" asked Lorna.

"Indeed. They caused quite the commotion in the forest when they interfered with the great mana vein. I thought the warning I gave them would be enough to keep them away. However...if Zariché's story is true, then it would seem they have continued their efforts to seize control of the forest. I suppose I am partly to blame for not realizing sooner..."

Even in town, Lorna had heard nothing but terrible things about her former family. They really did seem to be a despicable lot.

"Um... S-sorry about that...," she said.

"Worry not. Their sins are not yours to bear. Besides..." A harsh grin spread across the queen's face. "...They have chosen to disobey me despite my warning. And now I hear they have disrespected our benefactor. I think it's about time I put an end to that family."

"Oh, uh... Right."

In the past, the queen of the elves had signed a nonaggression pact with the countries of the human world.

The elven people's population was small, but they lived long lives. Even their common soldiers were incredible warriors skilled in magic, and all of them above Level 30. Even outnumbered, the elves could hold their own.

If an elf so desired, they were perfectly capable of doing as Zariché had planned and taking over the world.

The human leaders had no desire to make the elves their enemies. As such, the queen insisted that all they would need to do was to tell the human king about the mana vein's depletion and Zariché's schemes, and the humans would turn on the Guugelheits themselves without the slightest hesitation.

"Heh-heh... Those idiots have made a grave mistake. If only they had not been so foolish as to abandon their own daughter... They might well have seen riches beyond imagination. Heh... Heh-heh-heh-heh..."

Th-the queen's acting kind of scary...

Lorna felt ill at ease watching the queen chuckle malevolently. Discreetly, she put her hands together and offered a humble apology to her former estate.

After her conversation with the royals was over, Lorna and the elves continued their merrymaking.

Lorna got to enjoy elven delicacies the likes of which she had never seen, the children of the village all looked up at her with admiration, and the elven warriors asked her to join forces with them.

Once the party came to an end, the queen invited Lorna to spend the night at the castle.

"Oh? This board made of light... These are the words of the gods...?" asked the queen. "Nothing happens when I touch it."

"Those words were all written by the gods...?" Elna chimed in. "What do they say?! I can't read any of it!"

"Ngh...! To think, such hallowed words would be before my very visage, yet I am completely unable to read them...!"

"Ah-ha-ha...," Lorna chuckled weakly.

When she showed the internet to the queen, the normally dignified elf's eyes lit up like a child's as she struggled in vain to try to touch the window.

The internet was apparently a thing of unimaginable worth to a pious woman like Ellhar.

Meanwhile, Elna sat by her mother, watching her struggle with a look of slight embarrassment.

"And what of this?! Please, tell me what this says here!"

The queen reminded Lorna of a dog wagging its tail as she energetically pelted her with question after question.

"Um, this part that says 'lol,' you mean? That is grass."

"Grass? Why grass?"

"Well, in the language of the gods, it is customary to sprinkle little images of grass among one's words to indicate laughter. Sometimes the grass is more elaborate, with other shapes and letters, like little buds and flowers. The more letters one uses, the louder and more elaborate the laugh."

Lorna, who had become something of an expert on the internet, felt some measure of pride as she explained this and that to the queen.

"Hmm... I see! It seems the gods draw a comparison between the sound of laughter and the wind as it blows through the meadows. Quite the divine outlook indeed."

"Wow...! It's so poetic!" added Elna.

"Heh-heh... I suppose one might say that this situation is worthy of a whole meadow of grass lolololololol."

"Hee-hee! When I see the Savior, it makes me want to roll in the grass lololol!"

"Very good, Lorna! Grass all around lolololololol!"

The queen and princess continued to test out their newfound knowledge of internet slang long into the night.

Eventually, all this talk of "grass" would lead to a major commotion within the Hidden Village of the Elves. But that is a story for another time.

The next morning, the elves all gathered at the village gate to see Lorna off.

"You're really leaving, Savior?" they asked.

"Yes. I want to keep traveling. And people might start worrying about me if I don't get back to town soon."

She had told both Elmina and Reinharte that she was going to gather herbs, after all. And the family that ran the inn where she was staying were likely wondering why she hadn't returned.

"*Sob*... But, Savior..."

"If only you could stay with us in the village forever..."

The elves all hated to see her go—a stark contrast to their cold reception the day before. It was hard to believe they had all grown this fond of her in the span of a single day.

"I suppose this is not the ideal time to ask, but...are you certain you wouldn't prefer to stay with us in the village?" asked Queen Ellhar. "Though you may be a human, you are our Savior. You could spend your days here in peace. You would want for nothing."

"You're...probably right about that," answered Lorna.

"Then, you mean—"

"I'm sorry. I can't."

If Lorna had stumbled upon the village right at the start of her journey—before she had learned how to use the internet—then she might have accepted the queen's invitation without hesitation. Back then, survival was the only thing on Lorna's mind.

But thanks to the power of the internet, she had become stronger, eaten delicious food, gazed upon beautiful landscapes, met all sorts of people, and been thanked for helping them. Those experiences had made Lorna look inside herself and wonder what she really wanted. And what she found was the desire to be free to travel the world.

Until recently, Lorna had mostly stayed cooped up in her family's estate. That was partly because she was weak. But it was also because her family was hated all across the region.

Now Lorna was finally rid of her connection to the Guugelheits, and so...

"I want to live a life of freedom. There's so much I want to see. I want to eat all kinds of foods, meet all sorts of people... Once I've done that, I'll return. Someday."

Lorna wanted to try the local delicacies from every region, like Ipple pie and Elf crackers. She wanted to be moved by beautiful landscapes like the Twilight Temple and the Hidden Village of the

Elves. She wanted to master all manner of spells and skills. She wanted to make a bunch of new friends.

All these desires welled up inside her—there was just so much Lorna wanted to do!

"I...see. If that is how you feel, then it would be inconsiderate of us to stop you." The queen chuckled, then took the pendant necklace she was wearing and hung it around Lorna's neck. "In that case, I shall entrust you with this amulet. It is proof of your fellowship with the elven people. As long as you are carrying this, the humans you meet—be they noble or king—will receive you with courtesy."

"Um...are you sure? This thing looks pretty important."

"This is but a small token of our appreciation. A trifle when compared to all you have done for us." The queen jovially clapped her hand on Lorna's shoulder. "You are welcome in our village anytime. Our people never forget our debts. You are—now and forever—a friend to the elves. This land is and will continue to be your home."

"Thank you... I swear, I'll come back someday."

"Heh. I look forward to our reunion. May your travels be covered in grass."

After everyone had said their farewells, Lorna was finally ready to return to her journey.

""""Ready? One, two... Graaasss!!!"""""

That was the word the elves chose for Lorna's send-off.
And with that, Lorna left the Hidden Village of the Elves.

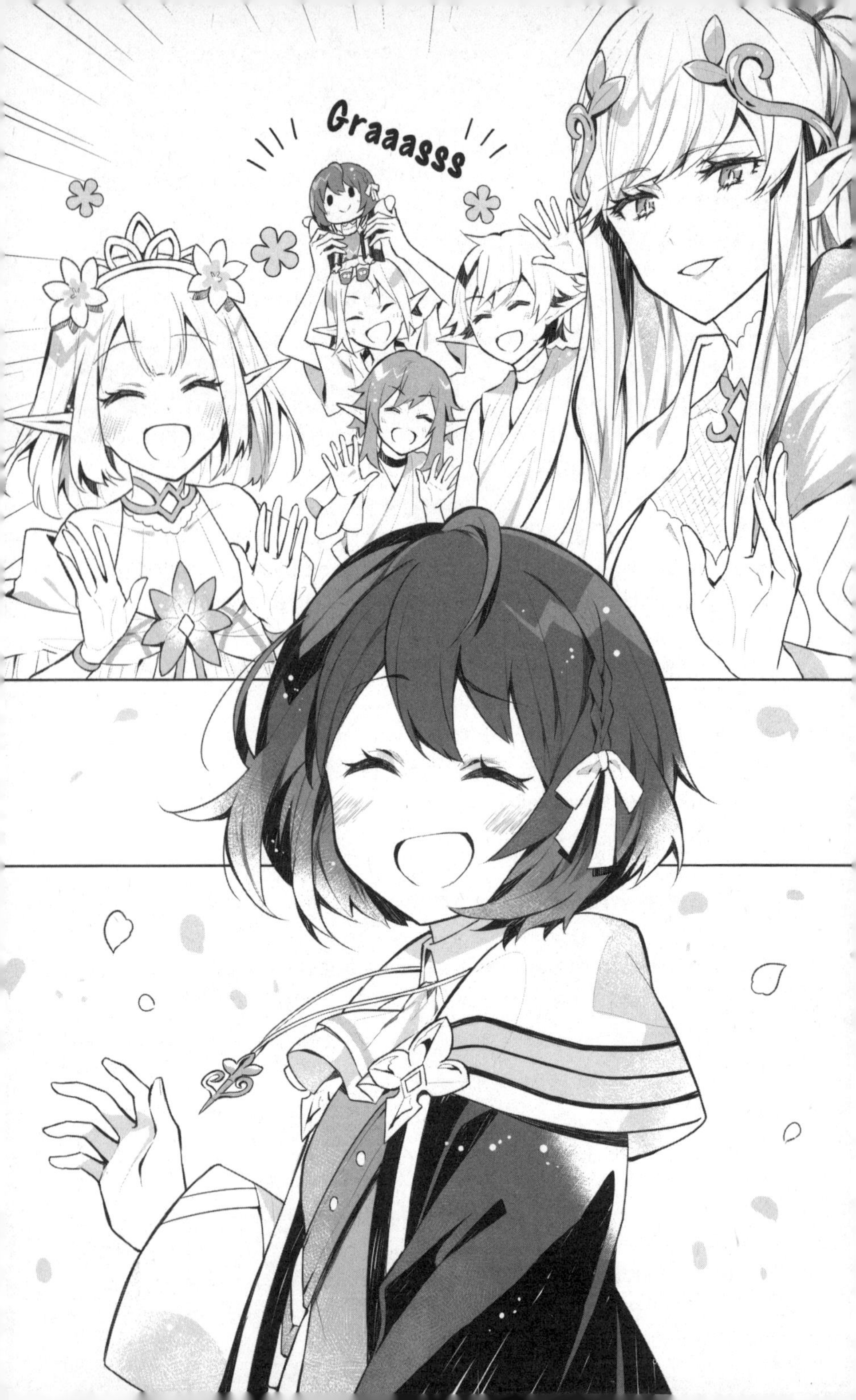
Graaaasss

Chapter 14 I Brought Back Souvenirs!

"L-Lorna! Are you okay?!"

When Lorna got back to Aiphoné, she found Reinharte at the gate. He called out to her in surprise.

Several other adventurers were gathered nearby, and they all watched in shock as Lorna descended from the sky.

"Oh, Reinharte. What's the matter?"

"Uh? What do you mean, 'What's the matter?' You disappeared into the woods for an entire day. I even gathered some people to go look for you…"

"Oh…"

The two of them had only just met, so Lorna hadn't expected Reinharte to be so worried. But then again, the woods were full of monsters, and she had shown no sign of coming home. It was only natural for him to be concerned, to say nothing of the natural disasters that had only just ravaged the area.

"Um… S-sorry about that…"

"No, no, don't apologize. I'm just…um, glad you're all right. I haven't had a chance to pay you back for all you've done for me, after all," Reinharte said with a chuckle.

"What happened in there? There are so many monsters, I assume you didn't try to sleep outside, right…?"

"Oh no, of course not. I got invited to the Hidden Village of the Elves. And they let me spend the night there."

"""" ...?!"""""

Lorna's words shocked everyone within earshot. Because she got all her information from the internet, she hadn't thought any of this was that big of a deal, but...

"Th-the Hidden Village of the Elves?! The one from the legends?"
"You mean you made it through the mists of confusion?!"
"Th-there's no way she's serious...right?"
"She *did* just descend from the sky..."

The adventurers gathered by the gate all murmured among themselves at this shocking revelation.

The Hidden Village of the Elves was famous among the adventurers in Aiphoné. Many hoping to strike it rich had tried to cross through the mists of confusion and find their way to the village. But every one of them without exception wound up aimlessly wandering the same area in circles.

Twenty years prior, the Guugelheits had sent their private army into the woods. But their entire force was wiped out before they could even reach the barrier.

Lorna hadn't heard about any of this, however, so she didn't understand why everyone was so excited.

"Oh, right! Here, I brought you back some souvenirs. I have enough for everyone, so you can all try some."

Lorna materialized a paper package full of Elf crackers from her Item Box and handed out the contents. According to the internet, it was the elven village's delicacy, so she thought it was worth sharing.

Everyone's gathered here for my sake... I'd hate to have them go home empty-handed.

That was the only thing on her mind as she casually handed out the crackers.

Chapter 14: I Brought Back Souvenirs!

The adventurers were once again left completely shell-shocked by this turn of events.

"What the—?! Where did that box just come from?!"

"Are you telling me that...these are the fabled elven sweets? I thought they only existed in stories."

"There's no way I can eat this... We should sell them. They must be as rare as a royal heirloom..."

"Hold on, hold on. You're not telling me you actually believe this girl's been to the Hidden Village of the Elves, are you?"

"Maybe we should get a scholar to take a look at these crackers and see what they think..."

The adventurers were completely absorbed in their lively discussion. For her part, Lorna was just happy that everyone seemed to be enjoying the crackers even more than she'd expected. This was her first time choosing souvenirs and handing them out, and she'd been a bit nervous about how well they would go over.

Looks like I made the right choice picking a snack that doesn't spoil quickly. I'm glad I read that Top 10 Tips for Buying Souvenirs They'll LOVE *page on the internet.*

Lorna, despite missing the mark somewhat, was completely satisfied with her conclusion.

Reinharte, meanwhile, looked confused. "Hold on... Something seems different about you, Lorna."

"Huh?"

"Uh, how should I say this? Something about you seems lighter, somehow. You look less stressed out."

"You think so? Hmm. I guess I am, now that you mention it. You might say I have a better idea of what I want to do with my life now," she said. Then something struck her. "Oh, that reminds me, Reinharte. Didn't you mention something about a strange illness that's been affecting the town yesterday?"

"Hmm? Oh yes. I do recall saying that. Why do you ask?"

Lorna suspected that Zariché's poisonous pollen had floated all the way to Aiphoné. But now that the source had been dealt with, everyone's symptoms were likely to improve.

"I don't think you have to worry about it anymore. Everyone should start feeling better in no time."

"Uh... What?"

Having said that, Lorna wandered into town, leaving Reinharte perplexed. After a few minutes of silence, something occurred to him. "...Wait! Did Lorna mean the whole reason she went to the Hidden Village of the Elves was to put a stop to the illness...? Hold on... This goes even further back. Now that I think of it, the natural disasters in the Ipple Woods came to an abrupt end just after Lorna arrived in Aiphoné... Has this been her plan the entire time...? To save the town...?"

The puzzle pieces all seemed to fall into place in Reinharte's mind.

"And despite all that, she doesn't brag about any of her accomplishments. Wow, Lorna... You really *are* amazing."

Slowly but surely, Reinharte had begun to see Lorna as a great and benevolent angel, come to save the people. Lorna, of course, was completely oblivious to this.

And speaking of Lorna...

Oh, right. I should go see Elmina and give her a souvenir.

...she was currently strolling through town, cheerfully thinking about her own benefactor.

Elmina had gone through so much trouble to re-re-reprint her adventurers card, and Lorna had been looking for a way to thank her. As such, she had resolved to give Elmina an *extra-special* souvenir.

Having made up her mind, Lorna wasted no time in finding Elmina.

Chapter 14: I Brought Back Souvenirs!

"Uh, let's see. I think her house is... Oh yep, here it is on the internet. All right. Enchanted Wings!"

Lorna sprouted wings of light and flew off in the direction of Elmina's home.

◇

Elmina Manaflame, the Witch of Conflagration. Nary a soul in Aiphoné did not know that name. She was an elite sorceress, the user of a rare A-Rank skill, and the young guild master of the Aiphoné Adventurers Guild.

Having aligned herself with the powerful Guugelheit family, she had lived her whole life as an elite among elites.

And right now, that elite sorceress was...

"...Okay. I'm done packing. Time to get the hell out of here."

...getting ready to skip town as fast as humanly possible.

She planned to flee Aiphoné at first light.

Sigh... I can't believe an elite like me is about to be homeless. Good-bye, elite lifestyle... If I stay here any longer, Lorna Hermit is sure to murder me. And I've already declared myself an enemy to the Guugelheits...

She'd been left with only one choice: to run away and never return.

So while Lorna Hermit was out of town, Elmina had sold her house (despite still owing money on her mortgage) and all her belongings. She had also left a letter announcing her resignation as the town's guild master.

But all of it would be worth it, as long as she could get away from Lorna Hermit.

"All right..."

Elmina used her Mana Scan skill to take a good look around.

"Lorna Hermit, Lorna Hermit... There she is—all the way over there."

Fwoooooooooooooooosh!!!

Off in the distance, Elmina could see a massive aura rising into the sky.

There was no mistaking that aura. Lorna emitted so much mana that Elmina could always get a precise read on her location.

Elmina would use that to her advantage and escape unseen.

Hee-hee... As if I'd let myself be intimidated by the likes of Lorna Hermit. I've secured multiple escape routes and devised countless scenarios to evade her. I've thought of everything. I am an elite, after all. And an elite like me does everything impeccably—even when it comes to skipping town.

Elmina went over her plan with a smug sense of self-satisfaction. But just as she was about to depart...

...What? Why does her aura look like it's heading this way...?

Fsssssshooo!!!

Lorna Hermit's terrifying aura turned and made its way straight for Elmina, traveling at tremendous speed.

W-wait... Th-this can't...

It was clear as day—the aura was cutting a straight path toward Elmina's home. It was almost as if the girl knew she was trying to beat a hasty retreat.

A moment later...

"Ohhh, Elmiiiinaaaa! ♪"

...Lorna came ripping through the air like a meteor, a huge smile evident. Seeing this, Elmina couldn't help herself.

I...can't take this anymore...

She fell to her knees in complete despair.

Chapter 14: I Brought Back Souvenirs!

Elmina welcomed Lorna into her house (which had already sold), as best she could.

Since she had already gotten rid of all her household furniture, Elmina offered the winged girl her own steamer trunk as a seat. Elmina, meanwhile, sat on the ground.

"U-um, is something going on? It looks like you're about to leave."

"...N-no. N-n-n-not at all..."

Elmina was already covered in cold sweat.

What is this...? What is she going to do with me? And why does she know where I live? My heart can't handle this...

The ex–guild master had no idea what to make of the situation, but she guessed that Lorna had come to warn her that she had no hope of escape. It made perfect sense—the girl had allowed her to do as she wished, but the instant Elmina tried to escape, she'd appeared as if from nowhere.

"Do you really think you can run?"

It was clear as day—Lorna was mocking her.

She's right...

Elmina already knew the terrible truth in her heart: There was no running away from Lorna Hermit.

Lorna, meanwhile, could see how upset Elmina was, and she was worried sick.

Oh no... Maybe it wasn't a good idea to look up her address on the internet and show up unannounced like this. Elmina's a kind person, so she's probably just humoring me. But by the looks of it, she was probably on her way out the door.

Lorna took a look around Elmina's empty home.

I'm surprised she lives such a simple life. I assumed that, as the guild master, she probably made a decent amount of money. Come to think of it, I bet she donates most of her salary to help out new adventurers. Just like when she covered the cost of printing me a new card over and over.

As Lorna sat there, head full of wild delusions, the elite sorceress finally spoke up.

"A-and to what do I owe the pleasure of your visit…? Are you here to tell me to end it all myself…?"

"Huh? End what now?"

Elmina's voice trembled as she tried to ascertain what horrible fate lay in store for her. Lorna, oblivious, suddenly remembered why she had come.

"Oh, right! Since I visited the Hidden Village of the Elves, I brought you back a little something."

"Th-the Hidden Village…*of the Elves*…?"

As usual, Lorna had casually name-dropped something only known in myths and legends. And that wasn't all.

"So without further ado… Ta-daa! Here's your souvenir."

Lorna pulled an item out of thin air as if it was the most natural thing in the world before handing it to Elmina.

The sorceress absentmindedly accepted the item. Then, taking a closer look, she realized it was a magnificent crown adorned with roses.

A…crown? But whose crown? I…have a bad feeling about this…

Elmina's hands began to tremble as she gripped the crown.

"Wh-what i-i-is it…?"

"The crown? Heh-heh! I got this in the Hidden Village of the Elves! Pretty great, right?"

"What… How…?"

"Oh, some enemy I beat up dropped it."

"Someone you *beat* dropped this…?"

"Yup!" replied Lorna with a big smile.

The truth was that it had dropped when she defeated the Queen's Heart Rose.

■ **Equipment (Head): Queen's Heart Crown**
Rank: B
Type: Helmet
Price: 8,700,000 shil
Effect: DEF +87, SPD +87, LUCK +87
Poison, Sleep, Charm resistance +87 percent
Draw Aggro (Large)
◇ **Equip Skill: Queen's Majesty (B)**
Effect: High chance of inflicting Charm on all lower-level enemies in range.

◇ **Details: Equipment dropped by defeating the Queen's Heart Rose.**
Despite being a crown, this helmet's stats and ability make it most suitable for a tank. It excels at rendering nearby enemies powerless, making it an incredibly useful piece of equipment for hunting or taming monsters. It's definitely worth grinding the boss until the crown drops.

I still don't get how a fully formed crown can just drop out of a monster like that… But it sounds like it's pretty rare, so I'm sure Elmina's going to love it.

It was a bit too gaudy for Lorna, who took one look at it and thought, *There's no way I'm walking around wearing this thing…* before sending it away to her Item Box. But a crown would be perfect for someone with a dignified air like Elmina.

Lorna watched for Elmina's reaction, a glint of expectation in her eye.

If the enemy she beat dropped this crown, does that mean…?

Elmina's body began to tremble in fear.

Has she committed regicide and usurped someone's throne…?

Elmina suddenly recalled the recent disaster that had befallen the Ipple Woods.

There was no doubt in her mind that Lorna was the culprit, but something else had caught Elmina's attention—she couldn't help but notice that a lot of the damage had taken place near the barrier created by the fog of confusion.

The elves were a cautious bunch. Surely, something so brazen happening near their village would be treated as an act of direct hostility.

And since there was no *official* way to enter the village without reaching a mutual understanding with the elves, Elmina could think of only one reason why Lorna would cause a ruckus so close to their border.

Was she trying to destroy the Hidden Village of the Elves…? Barrier and all…?

Everything clicked into place.

Surely, the "enemy" Lorna had mentioned was the elven people themselves.

Not even the Guugelheit family, all of whom were distinguished warriors, had been able to enter the village with their army. There was no way Lorna had gone into the village to defeat a mere monster or a thief—such weaklings would never had made it inside. And even if they did, the elven soldiers would quickly dispatch them.

And that meant there was only one possible conclusion…

"There were just *so many enemies* in the village when I was there. It was a real handful," Lorna explained. "Defeating all of them was so much work. I'd defeat one enemy, and another one would take its place… It took a lot to finally wipe them all out!"

Th-those poor elves…

"But thankfully, all the *enemies* I took out dropped a bunch of items. So in the end, I guess you could say I made a killing, heh-heh."

H-how is she so calm…? She just slaughtered and pillaged an entire village…

Chapter 14: I Brought Back Souvenirs!

"Plus, when I was done, the elves all offered me a bunch of jewels and food! These Elf crackers I brought back as a souvenir? They just *gave* them to me!"

Th-they must have offered them to get her to stop murdering their people...

"Oh, and the bed inside the elf castle? It was sooo comfy! I can't remember the last time I slept that well."

She's so...terrifying...

That was what happened when you opposed Lorna Hermit. And she'd recounted her deeds in such excruciating detail. The reason? That was obvious, at least to Elmina...

"Guess what, Elmina? You're next."

That was the only sensible conclusion Elmina could draw as she looked at the girl's grinning face.

"Um, Elmina? Why are you crying?"

"P-please...d-d-don't k-kill..."

"Huh? Don't kill *who*? My enemies?"

Lorna was perplexed. At first she didn't understand why Elmina was weeping.

Oh... I think I get it now. She probably pities all the monsters I had to defeat. She's like a saint. What a kind soul...

This made a lot of sense to Lorna.

In the end, for whatever reason, Elmina refused to accept the Queen's Heart Crown. Instead, Lorna opted to share some Elf crackers with her, taking care of the last of her souvenirs.

Unbeknownst to Elmina, Lorna had warmed up to her *even more*.

Chapter 15 I Left on a Journey!

"W-well then, M-Miss Lorna... These one hundred Phantom Leafs come to a total of five million shil..."

"Whooo!"

One week after returning from the Hidden Village of the Elves, Lorna paid a visit to the Adventurers Guild headquarters.

In the end, Elmina had decided to resume her post as guild master. She handed Lorna a bag stuffed with shil.

Lorna had harvested more leaves using the infinite duplication trick and brought them to the guild a week prior, but they'd sold for such a hefty sum it had taken a while to put together the money.

I'm just glad I was able to sell them all...

Lorna felt a sense of relief as she accepted her massive bag of cash.

Phantom Leaf might sell for a lot, but she wasn't sure how much of a demand there was for it. The leaf was practically on the level of an urban legend, after all. It rarely, if ever, found its way to the market.

When Lorna showed up to sell her wares, the employee at the guild had enthusiastically thanked her and said, "I'll buy every single one you have!" But when she pulled out a thousand of them, the employee got cold feet. "I... I couldn't possibly buy that many..."

This should be enough to get me started on my journey, though, so all's well that ends well.

The town of Aiphoné was under the direct influence of the Guugelheit family. Lorna, whom they had abandoned, wanted nothing more than to get as far away from their domain as she could, as quickly as possible.

Lorna was finally heading out, and that meant it was time for her to bid farewell to Elmina.

"I've decided to leave town," she said.

"...You have?" asked Elmina. "Really? Truly?"

"Yes, I'm afraid so. That's why I wanted to come here and say goodbye... Thank you for being so kind to me! I'll never forget you!"

"......"

Elmina stared at the girl, dumbfounded.

Uh... What? When was I ever kind to you?

Elmina was drawing a blank. As far as she knew, she'd only ever gotten in Lorna's way. And that meant the girl's words could only mean one thing.

"S-so... That's it, then...?" she asked. "Y-you've got no more use for me...?"

"Um. What?" Lorna stared at her blankly. She had no clue what Elmina was talking about.

What's that supposed to mean? Lorna wondered. *Uh, should I ask her? Oh no, there's a line forming behind me... Oh dear... If I don't say something, she'll think I'm being rude...*

And so...

"Eh-heh-heh... Yeah. I guess so!"

...Lorna gave her an innocent, noncommittal answer before turning around and making her way out.

"......"

Elmina stood for a moment in shocked silence.

"That's it... I'm done for," she moaned. "She's going to wipe me from existence..."

"Mistress Elmina, are you all right? M-Mistress...? Mistress Elmina! Are you unwell?!"

Chapter 15: I Left on a Journey!

A commotion broke out behind Lorna, but she was too focused on her own concerns to notice.

Okay, okay... Now that I've got some money, I can finally prepare for my journey.

Putting together everything she needed to set out on her adventure would cost, at minimum, thirty thousand shil. Originally, in order to get out from under the thumb of the Guugelheit family, Lorna was hoping to put together at least one hundred thousand shil. Right now, she had five million.

What's more, she still had about nine hundred Phantom Leafs in her Item Box—worth about forty-five million shil in total. Not that she could sell the whole lot of them all at once, mind you. But with this much money, Lorna could buy whatever her heart desired. She could even go on a gourmet tour of Aiphoné, just as she'd dreamed of doing when she first arrived.

Heh... Heh-heh-heh... I've got enough money on me... No harm in checking out a few of the food stalls before I leave, right?

Lorna made up her mind, wiped the drool gathering on her chin, and began her shopping spree.

She popped open a map on the internet and kept her eyes trained on it as she wandered from shop to shop. And as she did...

"Hyuk-hyuk-hyuk... You're Lorna Hermit, are ya?"

"No hard feelings, sweetie, but we got direct orders from the Guugelheits."

"Nothin' personal, but you're not leavin' this town alive, girlie."

Mmm-hmm-hmm! ♪ *What could be better than a gourmet tour of Aiphoné?* ♪ *Let's seeeee, where to next...?*

"*Take thiii—!* What the—? My sword broke on her!"

"Holy sh—! She's repelling my magic and my arrows!!!"

"C-calm down, stupid! It's *one* little girl. Let's all just rush her!"

* * *

If I store it in my Item Box, it looks like I can keep food fresh as long as I want... I might as well stock up on all the tasty treats this town has to offer before I leave! That way, I'll have all sorts of yummy stuff to eat during my trip, too. ♪

"Hi-yaaaaaah! G-gaaaahhh! My hand! She broke my hand!"

"Dammit, this chick's as hard as rock! Start pelting her with status ailments!"

"I-it's no good! Poison's not working! And I can't seem to blind her with Darkness or put her to sleep, either!"

Oh, darn it, another pop-up ad... Ugh... Why are these silly little Xs so hard to tap? ...Actually, hold on a second... This ad's kind of funny...

"She's laughing? She broke your hand, and she's *laughing*?!"

"Eep...! Wh-what the hell is this chick?!"

"Sh-she can't be human! I'm not letting a freak like her out of— Gyaaaaaah!"

"...Whoa!"

Lorna came to an abrupt stop. It seemed she'd accidentally bumped into someone. She must have hit the man pretty hard, because he'd been knocked to the ground. Trembling, he looked up at her.

"Oh my goodness! I am *so* sorry about that!" she exclaimed. "I didn't even see you there, and I—"

"You didn't even *notice* me...?!"

The man's body shook all over as he struggled to get to his feet.

"I... I can't do this! I can't deal with this monster! I'm gettin' the hell outta here!"

"Wh-whoa, what the hell?! Ya can't just leave us behind!"

"No... Nooooooo! Forget those damn Guugelheits; I don't want to die!"

The men around Lorna made quite the commotion as they ran off as fast as they could. She stared blankly after them as they disappeared into the distance.

"...I guess he was in a hurry," she said with a confused tilt of her head.

Whatever it was she had just witnessed, Lorna had learned a valuable lesson.

"I should stop staring at the internet while I'm walking. It's really dangerous!"

Not long after, Lorna finished preparing for her journey. All that was left was to chuck everything she'd bought into her Item Box.

When she first came to Aiphoné, she was worried that the Guugelheits would try something, but...

...I've had such a nice time here.

She had only spent about a week there, but she had come to love the rustic town and its simple pleasures. Of course, her fond feelings might have been inevitable—it was the first town she had ever visited, after all.

For now, she still wanted to put as much distance between her and her former family's domain as she could, but...

I'd love to come back here someday...once things settle down a bit.

Lorna wistfully held that thought in her heart as she prepared to move on.

"So...you're finally on your way, then?"

Lorna was at the town gate, saying her farewell to Reinharte. The guard looked at her like a lost puppy, left behind by its master.

"In my time as a guard, I've seen many people off on their journeys. Still, it always leaves me feeling lonely…"

"Well, I'm sure I'll be back someday, so don't get too down in the dumps."

"Well, then. Where are you planning to go first?"

"The capital."

Lorna had given a lot of thought to her destination over the past week, and she'd finally settled on the royal capital. There were lots of dungeons nearby, and she was sure to find plenty of jobs for an adventurer and nice spots to tour around.

What's more, as the old saying goes, "All roads lead to the capital." With so many highways spiraling out in all directions, it would be the perfect hub from which to visit other towns.

"My plan is to head to the capital and make that my base for future travels."

She didn't have any particular goal or final destination in mind. But she couldn't go wrong starting with the capital.

"I see. That does make sense. The monsters around the capital are quite strong, but I'm sure that won't be a problem for you."

"Right. Also, a relative of mine lives nearby…"

Lorna hadn't had much contact with her mother's side of the family, but she had met her aunt Millishira Hermit and her cousin Mina Hermit a number of times. She worried about how they might receive her now that she'd been ousted from the Guugelheit family, but she wanted to at least drop by and say hello.

She and Reinharte chatted at the gate for a while. Then, when Lorna was about to leave, he stopped her.

"By the way. I've decided to take the adventurers exam again," he announced. "I've been out of the game for five years now, so I'll probably have to start over from Iron rank… But once I join back up, I hope to meet you again somewhere, as a fellow adventurer."

"Of course! I'm sure we'll share lots of grass once we do."

"…Grass?"

They lapsed back into conversation for a while, until...

"All right," said Lorna. "It's about time I headed out."

"Indeed. I pray your travels will be full of joy."

Reinharte sent Lorna off with the same warm smile he had greeted her with when she first came out of the forest.

"Phew." Lorna sighed as she stood in the grassy plains outside town.

She couldn't quite put her finger on it, but her heart seemed much lighter now than when she had first arrived.

Come to think of it, I guess I'm way stronger than I was back then, she thought, popping open her status window.

■ **Lorna Hermit, Lv. 44**
  HP: 468/468
  MP: 99,999/288
  ATK: 46 (+360)
  DEF: 94 (+746)
  M-ATK: 181 (+3,600)
  MIND: 181 (+1,666)
  SPD: 92 (300)
  LUCK: 94 (+400)

◆ **Equipment**
  Weapon: Staff of World Tree (SSS)
  Armor: Apocalypse Dragon Ragnarobe (S)
  Armor: Reckless Boots (B)
  Accessory: Elf Queen's Amulet (A)
  Accessory: Substitute Doll (F)

◆ **Skills**
  Internet (SSS)
  Terra Drain (SSS)

Enchanted Wings (S)
Reckless Rush (B)
Magic VIII (D)
Giant Killer III (D)
Art of Slaughter II (E)
Dragon Slayer I (C)
Alchemy V (D)
Plant Killer I (F)

◆ Titles
The Abandoned One
Yggdrasil's Chosen
Calamity Witch
Lord Slayer
Apocalyptic Conqueror
Queen's Heart Rose Exterminator

"............Huh."

Perhaps Lorna shouldn't have checked after all. Whatever the case, she was strong. Even stronger than she'd realized. She felt like she was looking at some stranger's stats.

And to think that, just a week ago, I was struggling to kill a Slime...

Lorna's journey had begun only a few days ago. At this rate, what would her stats look like in a year?

Am I even still human...?

She tried to picture herself in the future, but the exercise only made her eyes glaze over. That said, a big part of her was excited to see where she would end up.

"...Anyway."

Lorna closed her stats screen and looked ahead of her.

Grassy plains sprawled out as far as the eye could see. A refreshing breeze was blowing, and the light around the sun formed a gentle halo.

She had enough money for her travels, and she had been freed from the confines of the Guugelheit estate. The world was Lorna's to explore as she wished.

Lorna took in a slow, deep breath. And then...

"Reckless Rush!"

...she activated her boots' equip skill, doubling her speed.

Then Lorna brought her fingers to her mouth and whistled as she sped off at a breakneck pace.

"Huuuuuh?!" Reinharte cried out in shock from behind her.

Anyone watching might think the girl had lost her mind. But according to the internet, this was a little trick called Whistle Sprinting—a movement technique passed down since time immemorial.

It really works, just like the internet said. As long as I whistle while I'm running, I'll never get tired! And I can avoid getting airsick from using Enchanted Wings. This is great!

And so...

"Fweeet... Fweeet... Fweeet...!!!"

Taka-taka-taka-taka-taka-taka-taka-taka!!!

Lorna raced across the grassy plains, kicking up a massive cloud of dust as she went. She was moving at double her normal pace, and even without the technique, Lorna's speed stat far outclassed that of any regular human.

She caught up with some other adventurers in the field, and they gawked at her as she tore past them like some kind of terrible speed demon.

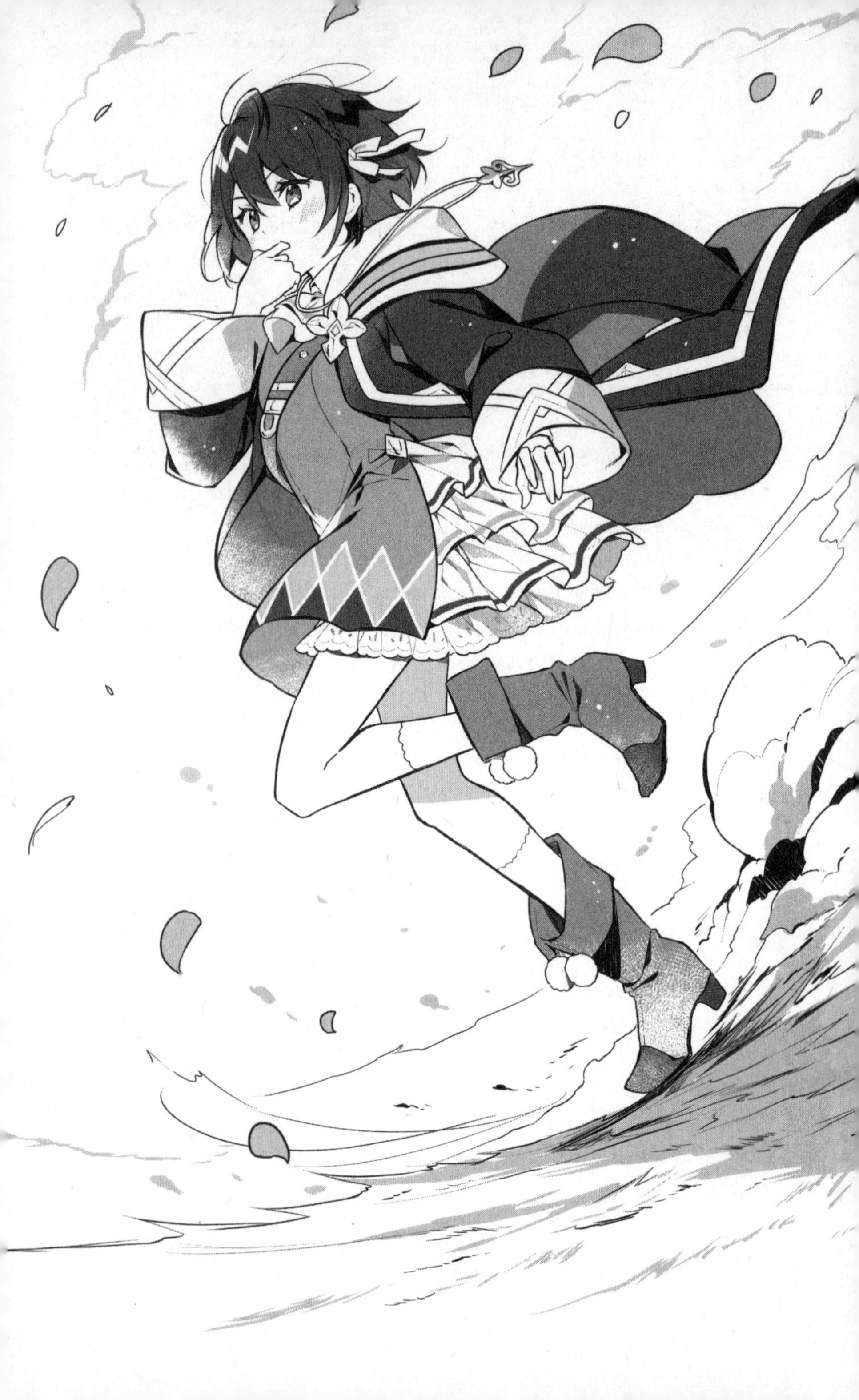

* * *

"What the heck was that?! Some kind of bizarre monster?!"
"Oh, her? That's the new girl, isn't it?"
"Yeah. Lorna Hermit. That's just how she is."

Satisfied with this explanation, the adventurers went back to their tasks.

"...She certainly was a strange one, right to the very end," muttered Reinharte.

Despite only being in town for a little over a week, Lorna Hermit had left an indelible mark on Aiphoné. She had changed Reinharte's life, too.

And as he watched her speeding off into the distance...

"...Pffftt... Ha-ha-ha-ha! Ah-ha-ha-ha-ha-ha!!!"

...the young guard fell into a fit of laughter for the first time in a very, very long while.

Chapter 16 Epilogue

Around the time Lorna was leaving Aiphoné, Margrave Brau Guugelheit sat in his estate, feeling rather vexed.

"Margrave... We can't take any more of this. We quit."

"Wh-what...?!"
A group of professionals were speaking through the communications crystal on Brau's desk. Each of them were high-ranked skill bearers the family had gone to great lengths to employ.
"H-hold on! What in blazes is going on?!"

"You can't be serious... You should know better than anyone!"
"You fed us false info and sent us after that damn monster!"
"You think our lives come that cheap, do ya?"

"Monster? What are you talking about?"

"Don't play coy with us! We're talking about Lorna Hermit!"
"A-are you stupid?! Don't say that name out loud! Call her 'the target' or something!"
"Yeah, what if she hears us?!"

*   *   *

"Wh-what...? You're not making any sense..."

Brau was growing increasingly confused.

Lorna Hermit...

That was the name of Brau's daughter. He'd ejected her from the family a week earlier for the sin of manifesting an SSS-Rank skill, the weakest rank imaginable. And now, for some incomprehensible reason, she was notorious in the town of Aiphoné.

The girl must have gone around telling everyone she was a Guugelheit, thought Brau. There could be no other explanation. How else could a weak vagrant like her become such a topic of conversation?

That was precisely why the margrave had sent men with skills suited to assassination to take care of her before she could besmirch the family name. And yet...

"Dammit! You've got some balls on ya sellin' us a line about the target only having some weak skill. Were ya trying to get us killed?"

"I've been sick of your crap for a while, but this is more than I can take. I'm done working with you lot. I'm outta here!"

"This is your mess, so you deal with it! I dunno what the hell you did to make enemies with a monster like that, but we're having no part of it!"

"W-wait, what are you—? H-hold on—!"

The communication ended before Brau could say anything else on the matter. For a while, he sat in confused silence.

"Wh-what is going on...?"

He began to tremble. This wasn't the first time he'd had to deal with one of his hired goons hanging up on him. High-ranked skill bearers had been defecting on him all day long.

"How...? How has it come to this...?"

A week ago, everything was going swimmingly. He had successfully convinced the A-Rank skill bearer Elmina Manaflame to become one of his retainers, and he was conspiring with Zariché

Venomgarden to bring the Hidden Village of the Elves to the brink of destruction. Everything was looking bright for House Guugelheit.

But ever since he'd kicked his daughter, Lorna, out of the family, it had all gone wrong.

The great mana vein had suddenly dried up. All manner of natural disasters had befallen the Ipple Woods. Elmina had betrayed him. Zariché's plan had been thwarted. And now the members of his army of high-ranked skill-bearing thugs were leaving in droves...

And amid all the commotion, one name came up again and again:

Lorna Hermit.

The daughter he had only recently abandoned in the woods.

Wh-why...? Wasn't her skill as weak as they come? It shouldn't have been possible for her to do away with our high-ranked skill-bearing retainers... Not with a lowly SSS-Rank skill like hers.

None of it made any sense.

But one thing was clear: Leaving Lorna to her own devices would mean trouble. She clearly had *some* kind of power at her disposal that was proving to be a thorn in his side. But treating her with open animosity was clearly not a winning strategy.

What if...I had her brought home? I'm sure if she were baited with the promise of returning to a noble life of luxury, she would come running of her own accord. And if she does have a useful skill, then I'll just have her use it for my sake.

The moment Brau devised this new plan, he contacted one of his underlings in Aiphoné.

"Listen up! That girl—Lorna. I'm calling off her assassination. Bring her to my estate at once!"

"B-but, Margrave Guugelheit...! I...believe that may be easier said than done..."

"You dare speak out of line?! If I tell you to bring her here, then you are to bring her here!"

"B-beg pardon... It's simply that...Lorna Hermit was spotted speeding across the fields outside town, whistling as she went. And, well, the speed at which she runs makes pursuit all but impossible!"

"What the blazes are you talking about?!"

"I don't understand it, either, Mar— Wait! What?!"

"What's the matter?! Answer me!"

"Lorna Hermit, she's... The girl has grown wings and has taken to the skies! Margrave, sh-she's flying!"

"Y-you're not making any sense, man!"

"I can't believe it, either, sir!!!"

It was no use—Brau couldn't understand anything these people were telling him. What was going on with that girl?

She's flying...? I've never heard of such a skill in all my days! If what they say is true, then that ability alone is worth bringing her back to the estate. But...how would we even apprehend her? If she leaves our domain, our people won't be able to give chase...

Brau racked his brain trying to come up with a plan. But before long, he was interrupted.

"Father! Come quick! There's trouble!"

The margrave's son Rowser burst into his chambers in a panic.

"What is it now?!"

"Th-the estate... We're surrounded! Royal knights! Elves!"

"Wh-whaaaaaat?!"

Brau screamed wildly as he ran to the window to see what was going on. He looked down and saw that countless elves had completely surrounded his home.

"Eeeeek!"

Even worse, while they were fewer in number, Brau could also see knights bearing the emblem of the royal family. That meant the king himself had ordered an attack on House Guugelheit.

Wh-what's happening—?! Don't tell me the king discovered my scheme to destroy the Hidden Village of the Elves! Or worse, what if he knows about what happened to the great mana vein?! Dammit! Whatever it is, how did he find out so quickly?!

Retribution had come far more swiftly than anticipated. The gathered forces were clearly here to eradicate the Guugelheit line.

"F-Father! We don't have much defense at the estate right now! We've no choice but to use our men as decoys while we flee underground!"

"Y-yes...quite."

Though the Guugelheits had many high-ranked skill bearers as their retainers, those forces weren't kept standing at the estate at all hours of the day. Aside from emergencies, the margrave had them take up important positions in the various towns of his domain.

At this rate, the elves and royal knights would easily overwhelm them with numbers alone.

But the elves haven't made any moves yet. If we escape now, we can ask for help from our...contact. They'll get us out of this bind...

Brau tore the carpet from the ground, revealing a stone staircase leading down to a secret passageway known only to a select few in the family.

Brau and Rowser had just begun the descent, when...

"Gyaaaaah?!"

"Rowser?!"

...the margrave's son let out a bloodcurdling scream that echoed up from the darkness. Then, in his place, a figure ascended the steps of this supposedly secret passageway...

"So...it seems the Savior was right. There truly was a secret passage here."

* * *

"…?! I-it's…you!"

A dignified elf in regal garb emerged from the shadows.

There could be no mistaking her. This woman was a hero spoken of in countless legends passed down through the ages. She was Level 70, the highest ever recorded in human history. And she was the very same warrior who had prevented Brau and his army from invading the Hidden Village of the Elves.

It was Ellhar, Queen of the Elves.

"Heh-heh… It certainly has been some time, little Guugelheit. Though I suppose at a time like this, the gods might say, 'Hiii, bestie'? Or perhaps, 'I weawwy missed u, uwu'?"

"Wh-what are…*you* doing here?!"

According to Zariché's reports, the queen had succumbed to her poisonous pollen and was unable to leave her sickbed. But now she looked as healthy as could be.

Brau cowered as the queen's quiet, knowing gaze pierced him to his core.

"Ngh…!"

He reached for a nearby sword, but…

"I suggest you not debase yourself in my presence."

The elven queen gently waved her staff.

Fwwwtssh!

Branches and vines grew out from the furniture in the room and, in an instant, wrapped themselves around Brau.

"Gaaah! Ng…nguhhh…"

The margrave was brought to his knees and bound in place. The powerful vines wouldn't allow him to move so much as an inch.

"Y-you…beast…!"

Brau was by no means a weak man. He was Level 40 and master of the B-Rank skill Mighty Sword. Most would view him as a strong warrior.

But the gap in strength between him and the elven queen was striking. He was like an infant facing off against a mature adult.

"Wh-why are you...?!"

"Heh-heh... 'Why,' you ask? A droll question if I have ever heard one. You harmed my people, didn't you?"

Queen Ellhar looked down at Brau, her eyes seething with rage.

"And now I am, as the gods say, 'big mad.'"

Fsssshhh!!!

The queen's murderous aura overwhelmed the margrave. It was enough to make the very air tremble. Glass and pottery around the room shattered instantly, and massive fissures opened up in the walls and floors of the mansion.

"Eeeek...!!!"

Brau began to sweat uncontrollably. He struggled to breathe, desperately gasping for air. In an instant, he lost all will to resist.

The difference in strength between the two was absurd.

That was when Brau finally realized something. It was something he should have figured out long ago.

One should never antagonize the elves.

"Hmph. In any event, I've come to see you today for one reason, and one reason alone: You see, the Savior of my people, Lady Lorna, is quite vexed by your existence. As such, I've decided to rid this land of your presence once and for all in order to make it more hospitable for her."

"Ngh...! Why?! Why do I keep hearing that girl's name everywhere?! And...Savior? Just what *is* that child?!"

"Hmph... Then it is true. You've no idea, do you? How ironic. To think that one who craves power above all else would throw their daughter to the wolves, only for her to become the world's strongest witch."

"Wh-what...? Lorna? The world's strongest witch? You must be joking..."

The elf queen looked down at the confused Brau with pity in her eyes.

"Foolish human. Had you not abandoned your daughter so easily, without even looking into her skill... If you had only let her cook, you might very well have had your shot to unalive me. You would no doubt be popping off at this very moment."

"I—I don't understand..."

"In other words: 'Lady Lorna is goated.'"

"G-goats? What are you...?"

Brau had been thrown into abject confusion. He couldn't figure out how it had all come to this. Nor could he understand the words coming out of the queen's mouth.

Everything was so bewildering. Could she be speaking some kind of ancient dialect?

"Now, then. This conversation has gone on long enough. It is time to end this."

"...D-dammit! Dammit, dammit, dammit! Damn it all to hell!!! My plan! It was perfect! This wasn't supposed to happen! It wasn't supposed to end this way! So...how?! *How the blazes did this happen?!*"

"You want to know, do you? Then I have just the thing to offer as a parting gift. If you wish to know how this all came to be..."

Ellhar then imparted the divine phrase Lorna had taught her.

"...just google it."

As those words left her mouth, the vines tightened around Margrave Brau's body and squeezed him until he lost consciousness.

The queen looked over her shoulder and called out, "It's over."

"Your Majesty! You have our gratitude for honoring us with your assistance!"

The royal knights cautiously entered the room and bowed low to Queen Ellhar.

She had sent one of her familiars to the human king and requested his help with the raid on the Guugelheit estate. She knew very well that, if the elves were to attack the House of Guugelheit without permission, it would be viewed as an international act of aggression. And so they had made sure to procure the king's blessing first.

Incidentally, she had decided to leave the family's punishment to the royal knights. She figured that, based on the nature of their craven acts, they were certain to at least be stripped of their rank.

"I—I never thought I would have the honor of meeting the legendary queen of the elves. Your Majesty has kindly helped us quell this conspiracy against our nation… We are truly in your debt."

"Heh… Then you would do well to remember this. In the language of the gods, one shows their appreciation by saying T Y, or the more formal T Y S M."

"…! The language of the gods?!"

"I-incredible…! I suppose I shouldn't be surprised that Your Majesty knows the divine tongue…"

"Heh. You are mistaken. I am not the incredible one—that epithet belongs to Lorna Hermit. She is the one who taught me these words. You also have her to thank for exposing the House of Guugelheit's crimes."

"Lorna Hermit? If she is a human worthy of Your Majesty's praise, then she must be truly formidable. Who is she?"

"Indeed. She is a girl capable of communing with the gods. An oracle and a savior. But more than all that—she is someone to whom my people owe a great debt."

"The oracle Lorna Hermit…"

"B-by the way. Would it be possible for Your Highness to teach us other phrases in the language of the gods…?"

* * *

"…kthxbai."

"…!!!"

The royal knights all scrambled to note down the queen's hallowed words.

And so it was that, unbeknownst to Lorna, word of the "Great Oracle Lorna Hermit" began to travel, along with the internet slang she had brought into the world. But that is a story for another time.

Keeping one eye on the royal knights as they apprehended Brau and Rowser, Queen Ellhar glanced around the room.

Let's see…

Her gaze fell on the communications crystal on the margrave's desk.

A magical implement… The technology is quite ancient. Between this and Zariché's Queen's Heart Rose seed…I smell something sinister afoot. The forces of darkness are beginning to grow in strength. It seems almost as if new enemies are being sent to our world from somewhere…outside of it.

After taking a moment for solemn thought, Queen Ellhar stopped herself with a chuckle.

But that is of little consequence… As long as Lady Lorna is with us, things are certain to turn out fine.

Lorna, the girl with the knowledge of the gods. With her in their corner, the idea of shadowy organizations plotting conspiracies seemed laughable.

That said, Lorna wasn't a fighter. If possible, Queen Ellhar didn't want to trouble her with such matters. And so…

"……"

The queen gently tapped her staff against the ground. In a flash, her army of elves appeared before her and knelt.

"If Lady Lorna's wish is to freely travel the world, then it is the duty of our people to help her achieve that. So, my elven warriors—spread across the land and support her from the shadows. Do I make myself clear?

""""Yes, Your Majesty!"""""

And with that, her army dispersed.
Each of them was among the strongest warriors in the world—Level 30 to 50, all. They were certain to prove useful to Lorna.
It was time for the elves, who had long kept out of the public eye, to venture forth into the world once more.

Side Story Registering to Be an Adventurer

"Um, I think I can register here."

Shortly after arriving in the town of Aiphoné, Lorna took Reinharte's advice and headed to a building bearing the mark of the Adventurers Guild.

■ **Map: Aiphoné—Adventurers Guild Headquarters**
Players who begin their journey in Aiphoné will take their adventurers exam in this building.
All the quests are beginner-friendly, and there are a number of manuals available that offer combat tutorials.
Most of the main and side quests early on in the game are issued from this location, so if ever you get lost, this place should be your first stop.

It's right where the internet said it would be.

Lorna looked at the map again. There was no mistaking it—this was the Adventurers Guild headquarters.

That was all well and good, but...

"There's been a disaster in Ipple Woods?!"
"What's going on over there?! The terrain has been completely altered!"

"I heard all the monsters have been hunted to extinction!"
"The Lord of the Woods... I can't sense it anywhere..."
"Does this mean the Demon Lord's been revived?!"

These people... They're blocking my way...
Lorna was stuck standing at the building's entrance. It was chaos inside. The doors had been flung wide open, and droves of adventurers were screaming at each other as they ran back and forth. The atmosphere was positively brutal.

One thing was clear, at least: Lorna's "natural disaster" was the cause of the commotion.

Welp... Guess I'll forget about becoming an adventurer.
She was already feeling ready to give up. But if she didn't become an adventurer, she couldn't make any money. It was the only surefire way for a traveler to save up the shil they'd need to continue their journey.

A-anyway, as long as I try my best not to stand out, it should be fine...
Lorna kept her head down and quickly moved through the crowd into the building.

But despite her attempts to avoid the others' gazes...

"...Geh-heh-heh. Get a load of that fancy staff. Must've cost a fortune."

"That's definitely combat gear. Which means she's not here to issue a quest..."

"Tale as old as time. Some noble's kid gets Daddy to buy her a fancy weapon and thinks that makes her an adventurer."

"In other words...this girl's probably got more shil than she knows what to do with."

They whispered and laughed as she walked by.

She looked for all the world like a naive little girl. To the group of delinquent adventurers, she was the perfect mark.

"You thinkin' what I'm thinkin', Chumpo?"

"Geh-heh-heh... Like you even gotta ask."

Side Story: Registering to Be an Adventurer

Three large men stood up and headed toward Lorna.

The other adventurers and guild staff merely stood by, trying not to get involved. Normally, industry veterans would have stepped in to put an end to the men's crooked schemes, but every one of them was out investigating the cause of the natural disasters.

And so the three large men approached Lorna and stood in her way.

"Geh-heh-heh! Well, well, little lady— Eeeeee?!"
"We're not gonna let you pass— Ahhhhh!"
"Give us all your money— Eeeeee?!"

In the end, all three of them were run over. The instant they made contact with Lorna, they were sent flying across the room. They felt like they'd been hit by a runaway carriage.

"""GUH?"""

Everyone in the room fell silent, then turned and gawked at Lorna.

Lorna, meanwhile, was just as shocked as everyone else.

Uh... Why did the people I bumped into go flying across the room?

Lorna had recently ascended to Level 22—putting her in the same league as some of the most skilled adventurers. And the gear she had equipped brought her ATK and SPD stats over 300. She had yet to fully realize the ramifications of these changes.

Even setting aside her outrageously high MP and M-ATK, Lorna had one of the highest physical attack stats in the kingdom. The men might have been large, but they were still weak, and they'd made the grave mistake of trying to impede Lorna mid-power walk.

"Wh-whoa... What the...?"

The other adventurers quickly came to a realization: This girl's stats were off the chart. They all shared the same thought at the same time.

What the heck is up with her...?

This would later become the starting scene of a new tale in Aiphoné known as the "Legend of Lorna, the World's Strongest Witch." But at the time, Lorna had no way of knowing that.

"U-um, are you all right...?" she asked. "Sorry I accidentally sent you flying across the room..."

"O-oh... Err... I-I'm f-fine..."

"You're...here for the adventurers exam...right?"

"Th-the reception desk is...over there."

"...Oh? Thank you." Lorna was confused, but she headed in the direction the nice men had pointed.

I don't really get what just happened, but they seemed kind. Come to think of it, I bet they put on that little comedy performance to help set new adventurers at ease!

The Adventurers Guild was a lot less scary than she'd anticipated.

But Lorna didn't have time to worry about that. She had important business to take care of.

"Um, hi there," she said to the clerk. "If you don't mind, I'd like to exchange these materials for shil..."

"Hmm? Oh! Yes, of course. Would you show me what you've brought, please?"

"Okay."

Lorna rifled through her bag and pulled out one thing after another. Gems and materials, and more gems, and more materials.

"...?!"

Soon, the desk was covered with all sorts of drops from what must have been powerful monsters (the clerk hadn't seen much of it before and couldn't be sure), and what looked like the fabled

Phantom Leaf, which was said to grow only in very small quantities in the Magic Forest.

What the heck is up with this girl...? The clerk's face twitched as she tried to maintain her composure.

"Oh, also, I'd like to, um, register as an adventurer... Is that the right word?"

"...You mean...you're not registered yet?"

"...Huh? Well, no. Is that a problem?"

"You're telling me you're not even an official adventurer and you've still gathered this much stuff...?"

"Oh, uh, y'see... I was just walking along in the woods. And wouldn't you know it, I found a bunch of gems just lying around! I guess it was my lucky day."

That made everything even stranger. A person didn't simply *walk along in the woods* all alone when the place was crawling with monsters. Usually, you needed someone to scan for enemies, someone to carry gear, someone to fight... Handling all that by yourself was practically impossible. And now this girl was casually claiming that she'd done just that. Like it was no big deal.

"V-very well... Allow me to scan your stats for a moment, if you would. Please place your hand on the stats tablet."

"Oh... Okay."

Lorna unequipped her staff and placed her hand on the stone tablet. The next moment, a display popped up and revealed her stats to the clerk.

Wh-what?! Level 22?! And her speed...364?! This innocent-looking child? Come to think of it, wasn't Lorna Hermit the name of the girl Miss Elmina told us to take into custody the moment we spotted her?

The clerk looked back up at Lorna. She appeared to be an average, empty-headed girl. Or at least she did at first glance. But the clerk had seen many adventurers come and go in her day, and she could tell one thing for sure— Something *wasn't right* about this girl.

No way am I getting involved with this... Better pass her off to Miss Elmina.

The woman behind the counter pulled out a registration form. In the box labeled RESPONSIBLE PARTY, she wrote *Elmina Manaflame*.

With that, Lorna was ready to start her adventurers exam, unknowingly kicking off a period of great suffering for Elmina.

Afterword

Hello there, my name is Mochimaru Sakaki!

Thank you so much for taking the time to read this story! I'm so glad that I get to meet you all like this!

For this series, I wanted to answer the question: What if a character from a game world had access to a walk-through site?

But I didn't actually start with that idea. At first, all I was thinking was, "I'd love to write a story about a witch," and "It's been a while, so maybe I should write a comedy," and also "I want to write a story about journeying through a game world." And while I thought all those things, I tried out a few different story elements until I finally settled on the one you've just finished reading.

By the way, I just looked, and I wrote the first forty or so pages of this book back in April 2021. It's scary how fast time flies. I can't believe it's already almost 2022…

Anyway, that's the tale of how this book came together. I just hope that all you readers out there have enjoyed it.

Finally, a few words of thanks.

I would like to thank everyone on the SQEX Novel editorial team.

I'm so grateful for all the hard work you put into making this novel a success, despite the difficulties of COVID-19.

Incidentally, this is the first time I had one of my stories novelized after bringing it directly to the editorial department... And since I'd never had this sort of experience before, I was constantly thinking, *I really hope this is okay* and *I hope I'm not being a bother.* I was very nervous, but about a week after my submission, the editorial team sent me a long, thoughtful email with their comments and said, "We'd love to turn your story into a novel!" I'm so grateful.

I would also like to thank riritto for drawing the illustrations in this volume.

Thank you so much for creating such cute and incredibly detailed images!

To be honest, when I heard riritto mentioned as a possible illustrator for the series, I thought, *Whoa, I've totally heard of them...* I was practically trembling. I still can't believe they wound up taking on my story! In fact, not long before, I had been looking at one of riritto's covers and thinking, *This illustrator is so amazing. I'd love it if we could work together sometime.* I was practically daydreaming about it. I was so surprised when it actually happened.

And once I saw the illustrations, I was even more shocked by how spot-on all the characters were! And then I saw just how sparkly (?) the cover was and the look on Lorna's face when she summoned the dragon of flames; it was all just so perfect...

I know I asked you to include a lot of troublesome details and setups in the illustrations (I'm really sorry about that!), but I am just so, so grateful that you read the text as carefully as you did to get everything right.

* * *

And finally, a special thanks to all my readers.

Currently, Kodansha plans to release a manga of this story as well, and I intend to continue working hard to make it a fun series, so I hope you'll keep reading.

Mochimaru Sakaki

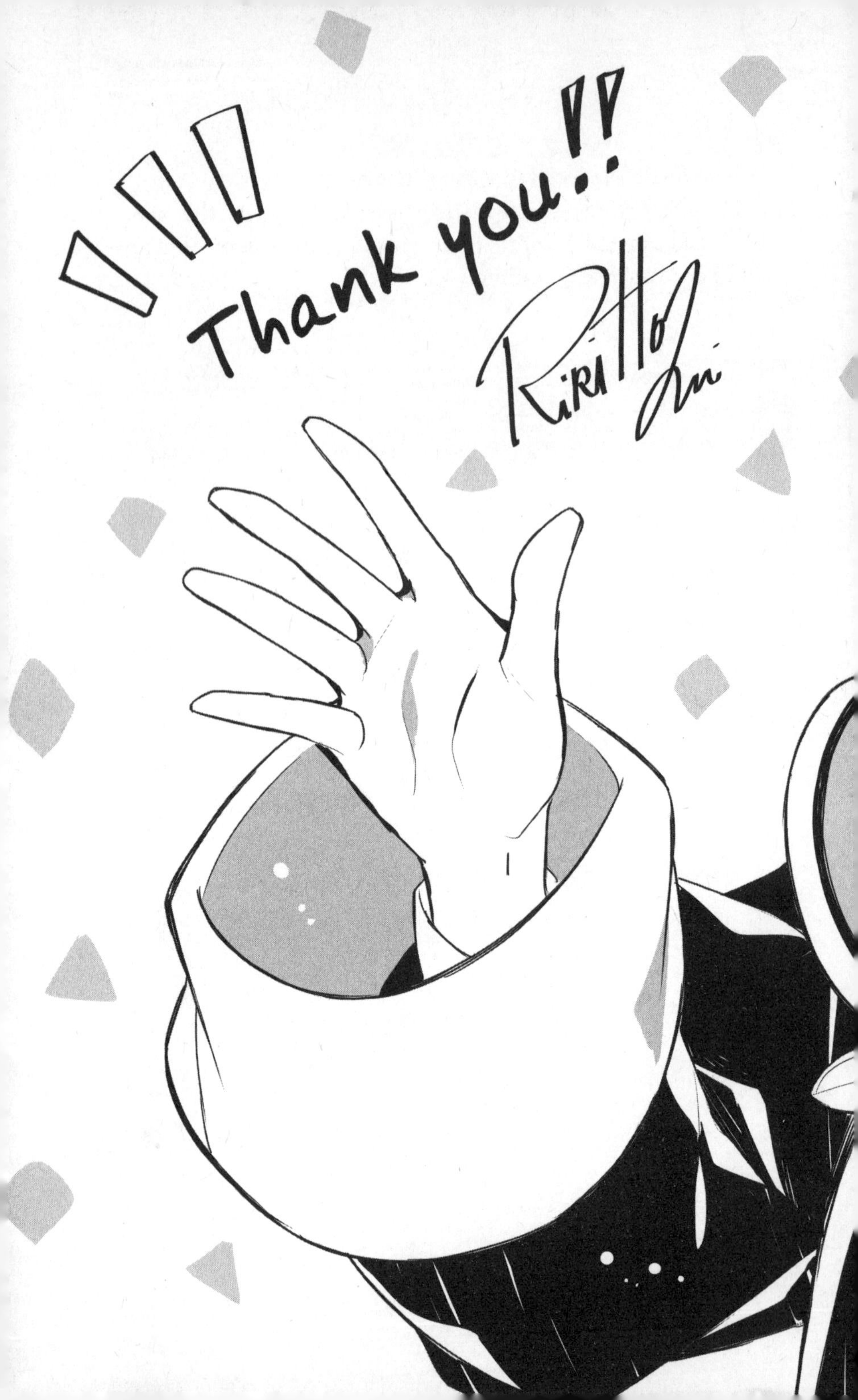

Thank you!!

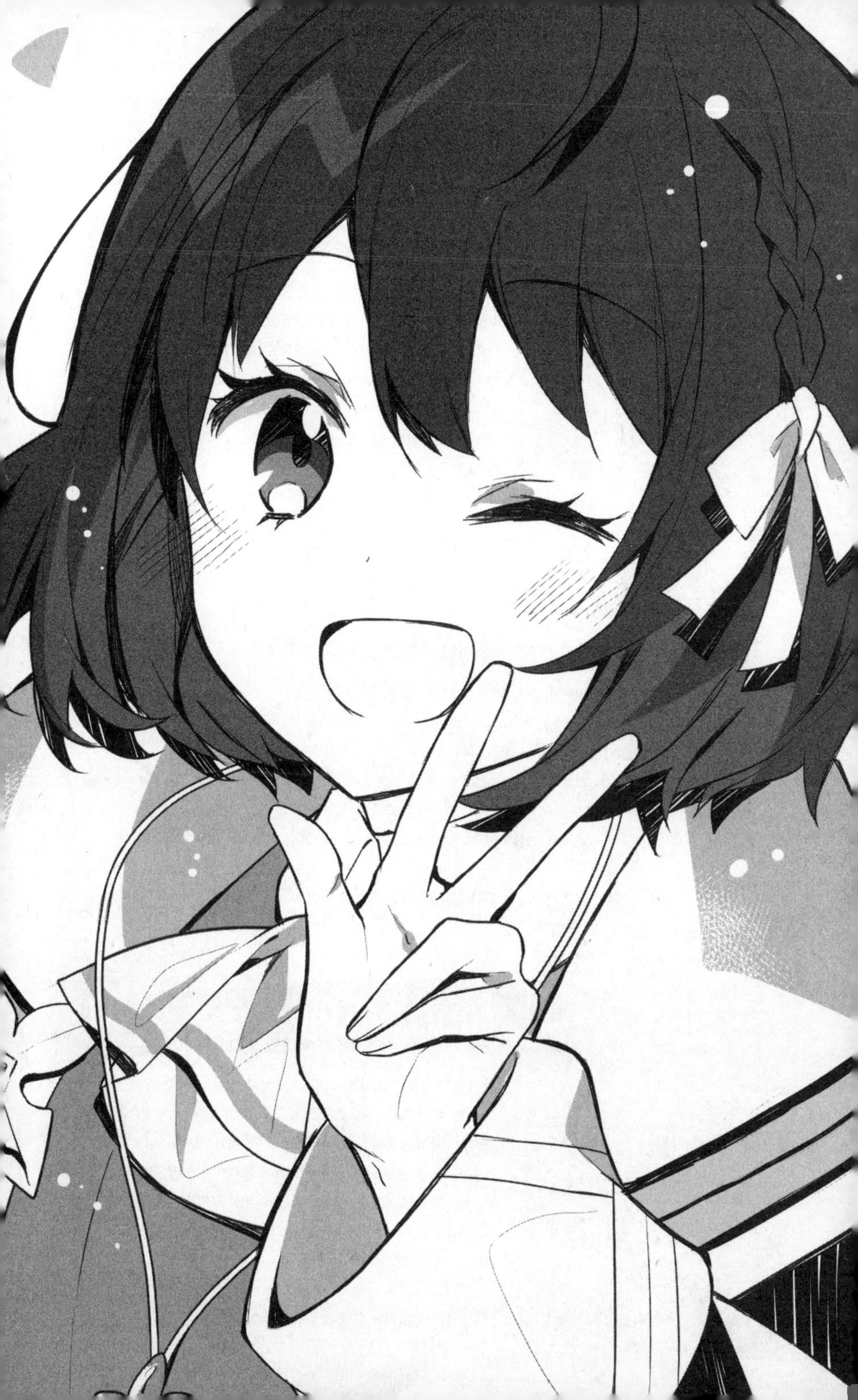

HAVE YOU BEEN TURNED ON TO LIGHT NOVELS YET?

86—EIGHTY-SIX, VOL. 1–13

In truth, there is no such thing as a bloodless war. Beyond the fortified walls protecting the eighty-five Republic Sectors lies the "nonexistent" Eighty-Sixth Sector. The young men and women of this forsaken land are branded the Eighty-Six and, stripped of their humanity, pilot "unmanned" weapons into battle...

Manga adaptation available now!

WOLF & PARCHMENT, VOL. 1–10

The young man Col dreams of one day joining the holy clergy and departs on a journey from the bathhouse, Spice and Wolf. Winfiel Kingdom's prince has invited him to help correct the sins of the Church. But as his travels begin, Col discovers in his luggage a young girl with a wolf's ears and tail named Myuri, who stowed away for the ride!

Manga adaptation available now!

SOLO LEVELING, VOL. 1–8

E-rank hunter Jinwoo Sung has no money, no talent, and no prospects to speak of—and apparently, no luck, either! When he enters a hidden double dungeon one fateful day, he's abandoned by his party and left to die at the hands of some of the most horrific monsters he's ever encountered.

Comic adaptation available now!

THE SAGA OF TANYA THE EVIL, VOL. 1-14

Reborn as a destitute orphaned girl with nothing to her name but memories of a previous life, Tanya will do whatever it takes to survive, even if it means living life behind the barrel of a gun!

Manga adaptation available now!

SO I'M A SPIDER, SO WHAT?, VOL. 1-16

I used to be a normal high school girl, but in the blink of an eye, I woke up in a place I've never seen before and—and I was reborn as a spider?!

Manga adaptation available now!

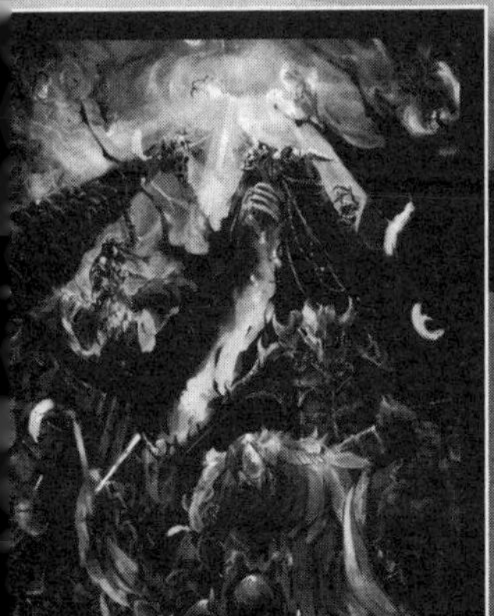

OVERLORD, VOL. 1-16

When Momonga logs in one last time just to be there when the servers go dark, something happens—and suddenly, fantasy is reality. A rogues' gallery of fanatically devoted NPCs is ready to obey his every order, but the world Momonga now inhabits is not the one he remembers.

Manga adaptation available now!

VISIT YENPRESS.COM TO CHECK OUT ALL OUR TITLES AND...

GET YOUR YEN ON!

I've Been Killing Slimes for 300 Years and Maxed Out My Level

It's hard work taking it slow...

After living a painful life as an office worker, Azusa ended her short life by dying from overworking. So when she found herself reincarnated as an undying, unaging witch in a new world, she vows to spend her days stress free and as pleasantly as possible. She ekes out a living by hunting down the easiest targets—the slimes! But after centuries of doing this simple job, she's ended up with insane powers... how will she maintain her low key life now?!

IN STORES NOW!

Light Novel Volumes 1-15

SLIME TAOSHITE SANBYAKUNEN, SHIRANAIUCHINI LEVEL MAX NI NATTEMASHITA
© 2017 Kisetsu Morita
© 2017 Benio / SB Creative Corp.

Manga Volumes 1-13

SLIME TAOSHITE SANBYAKUNEN, SHIRANAIUCHINI LEVEL MAX NI NATTEMASHITA
©Kisetsu Morita/SB Creative Corp.
Original Character Designs:
©Benio/SB Creative Corp.
©2018 Yusuke Shiba
/SQUARE ENIX CO., LTD.

For more information, visit www.yenpress.com